GOODBYE, BUFFALO SKY

GOODBYE, BUFFALO SKY

BY

John Loveday

MARGARET K. McElderry Books

MARGARET K. MCELDERRY BOOKS
25 YEARS • 1972–1997

Margaret K. McElderry Books
An imprint of Simon & Schuster Children's Publishing Division
1230 Avenue of the Americas
New York, NY 10020

Book design by Michael Nelson

The text of this book is set in News Gothic.
Printed in the United States of America
10 9 8 7 6 5 4 3 2 1

Library of Congress Cataloging-in-Publication Data:
Loveday, John.
Goodbye, Buffalo Sky / John Loveday. —1st U.S. ed.
p.   cm.
Summary: Cappy, who lives on the American frontier in the 1870s, must fight for the people
he loves, including an Indian woman from the Mandan tribe.
ISBN 0-689-81370-8
[1. Frontier and pioneer life—West (U.S.)—Fiction. 2. West (U.S.)—Fiction. 3. Mandan
Indians—Fiction. 4. Indians of North America—Great Plains—Fiction.] I. Title.
PZ7.L9560355Go   1997
[Fic]—dc21
96-45402
CIP   AC

To A. C. and P. B.

CONTENTS

Chapter 1

SPYING

"Come out of there."

I crouched quickly, my heart thudding. I waited for the order to come again. There was no sound, apart from a whinny from Burkhart's horse, like it had been scolded.

A bit of time passed. I wondered if it was safe to move. I looked up at the cobwebbed window, but decided to stay down, even if there were spiders. So I made myself more comfortable by dropping onto one knee.

"Are you coming out of there?" Burkhart called after a long while.

I glanced around the derelict cabin, to the broken door at the back, and realized that my thoughts of running out and away, instead of facing Burkhart, were foolish. I liked the man and knew that he liked me and I didn't want that to change. I knew that I must go out, walk around the side and into the open, and face what I had to face.

The cabin was near the bottom of the slope. As I came out into the sunlight, I hesitated, then walked toward the man, the horse, and the girl. I noticed again how the shadows under the birch trees half hid them. But here I was, walking toward them, with nowhere to hide. My face burned with shame.

Burkhart did not stop drawing. The Indian girl sat on the white horse, facing somewhat away. She was naked except for her dress folded across the front of the saddle. I knew that my shame was not only at being caught spying but in spying on a scene that was private.

I stopped a little way off, but my shadow fell on the sketchbook page. Burkhart kept on drawing, but gestured me to move aside. I sidestepped. The girl did not even turn.

She was deeper into the shadows. I wasn't sure if it was okay to look. Her golden skin was changed by light and shadow to different colors. They flickered and changed in the moving light, as the leaves moved, and I must have stared for longer than I knew.

"Here. Draw."

Burkhart was holding out his sketchbook and pencil.

"I . . . I . . . can't."

"Draw."

His voice was sharp, but his eyes looked amused.

"I can't."

"Do you ever draw?"

"No."

"Then how do you know you can't?" He waited, then said, "It is what I expect as your penance for dishonesty."

"I ain't dishonest."

"Oh, *ain't* you? Hiding yourself to spy on me is dishonest, isn't it?"

"I guess so. I'm sorry."

"Draw."

But the girl looked back and said something in her own tongue. Burkhart replied, laughing. She put on her dress and jumped down. She put an arm around the horse's neck, from underneath, her head against his shoulder, and smiled to us shyly.

My shame was suddenly gone, and what I said took me by surprise. "Your wife is beautiful."

"She is also modest, and you must go."

"She is beautiful," I said again.

I didn't mean to say the words. They just spoke themselves.

He smiled. "So you're glad you spied?"

We looked at each other before I looked down, and he knew what I was thinking.

"Well, you're no longer dishonest. And another day I might start to teach you to draw."

He opened the sketchbook and stood looking at a

drawing. I could see that it was of his wife on the horse, but he closed the book without showing me.

"Yes, she's beautiful," he said, "and modest. Her name is Two Songs."

In the early evening, from my bedroom window, I saw the white horse coming over the hill toward the settlement, Burkhart riding at a canter, with Two Songs behind him, clinging to his waist, her long black hair flying. I stood at the mirror for a while, wondering how I had looked to her as she smiled from the horse's shoulder. Later, I found I could imagine her smiling in the darkness as I dropped toward sleep.

Chapter 2

FRIENDS AND STRANGERS

I lived with Bessie Bell. She told me how she took me in as a kindness to my father. He had lost my mother, she said, out on the prairie, miles from anywhere. For a long time I thought "lost" really meant that somehow they had not been able to find each other, and sometimes I used to think of her out there wandering in tall grasses that stretched into the distance for ever. When I understood what the word really meant, I tried never to think about it, but that vague figure still moved in the grasses of my mind. My father had gone westward, and my thoughts of him were of a man in dark streets beyond mountains at sunset. Nothing more. I tried to imagine a face, but no face came. I looked in the mirror and tried to think of my face as it might be years from now, lined and weathered, but only the face of my twelve years looked back. I liked that well enough, but wished my fair hair darker. Sometimes, getting ready for school, I wet it a bit from the pump in the yard and made a temporary change that Bessie said looked ridiculous.

"Heavens, you look like a travelin' pantie salesman," she chided.

We lived in two rooms in the Eldo house. They were only bedrooms, and we ate downstairs with the family and any paying guests. Sometimes there were no guests; at other times the house was crowded, strangers content to pile into rooms with several others simply to get a roof over their heads. Often, in the morning, they were not so content, and when they had gone Mama Eldo would retell complaints about the snorers, smellers, coughers, swearers, that made up the part of the human race that passed under her roof. There were other complaints she only mentioned when her two girls and I had been told we could leave the table, so we never knew what they were. "Indecencies," the older girl, Alice, who was thirteen, confided. When I asked what she meant, she said, "How would I know?"

I was beginning to like Alice more.

"Cos she's gittin' titties," said Hurley. He said it was always that way with girls.

"It ain't that they git any better. It's jest that you don't git so mad at their perculities."

"Their *what?*"

"Their perculities."

"What's them?"

"Obvious," said Hurley.

I didn't see that it was obvious, so I asked Bessie what perculities were.

"You bin listenin' to Hurley," she said. "That's a Hurley word. He means 'peculiarities.'"

I said, "Oh," and went out before she could ask what Hurley had been telling me. She was not sure that I should spend as much time as I did with Hurley. He might be a bad influence. He had spent too long as a soldier, and getting his leg wounded had made an odd man odder.

Hurley lived in the outhouse, where the wood was stored and where Mama Eldo did the washing in the big copper tub. He came into the house at mealtimes, except when there were guests, when he collected his food at the kitchen door. He made a little money by doing digging jobs around the settlement, but he could never afford to pay for more than the food he ate. Bessie said he was lucky that Mama Eldo had lost one of her brothers in the war, and so could sympathize with him.

"You show them how tall you really are, Hurley," Mama Eldo would say sometimes, in front of strangers. Hurley would grin and stand straight on his good leg, making the crooked one swing back and forth a surprising way clear of the ground. Then, when paying their bills, departing guests might leave a few extra coins.

"And give this to the poor fella with the leg," they said.

It was around the time that I was beginning to be easier with "perculities" that Burkhart arrived back from his long painting trip into Indian country, bringing his beautiful wife, who seemed maybe no more than a couple of years older than Alice.

Chapter 3

DISTANT GUNFIRE

Two Songs was putting up a tepee on the spare ground beside Burkhart's cabin. It seemed that everyone in Buffalo Sky came out to watch.

"It's their way," someone said. "Let the squaw do the work."

"Good idea," said Hurley. "'Bout time we tried it."

"'Bout time you got on with diggin' my new latrine," said Dolly Emms, the storekeeper. "I bin waitin' a month. Wait much longer, you'll be diggin' my grave."

Hurley spent most of his working days digging himself down into the earth, for latrines, graves, ditches. It was very usual to hear him call his "Hi, there, Cappy!" from some low level, only his untidy hair, brown face, and grinning teeth visible.

Burkhart was only watching his wife like the rest of us. She wanted the pride of doing the job herself, in the way all Indian women did. The tepee would be hers. We would come into it as her guests.

"Perhaps you will be the first," Burkhart said. "She likes you."

After the poles came the buffalo hides, decorated with pictures, some of which Burkhart had painted when he had stayed as a guest in a Sioux encampment many miles upriver. Up near the opening where the poles were crossed, there was a band of blue, with stars and a moon. Lower, figures of Indians were hunting, running, dancing. At the bottom, near the entrance, was Two Songs' pony. Further around, was the white horse.

Hurley came hoppity-hop over to Burkhart.

"One or two ladies is objectin', Mister Burkhart. You painted your horse too much stallion."

"He *is* a stallion."

"I know that, an' Cappy knows that, but Dolly Emms she don't seem to think it right that folk generally should know," said Hurley. He grinned. "Kinda disgustin', she say."

Burkhart was amused. "People are easily disgusted."

Hurley was thoughtful for a moment. He had that faraway look that sometimes came into his eyes.

"You're right 'bout that, Mister Burkhart. But they git disgusted 'bout the wrong things."

Hurley went hop-hoppity away toward the other bystanders, but passed them and went on along the road. I

noticed that he had picked up his spade from somewhere. Maybe he was going to dig Dolly Emms's latrine.

"Poor Hurley," said Burkhart. "Always a sound of distant gunfire around him."

Burkhart had once told me how he himself had been
in the war, but not as a soldier. He had worked as a nurs-
ing orderly among the wounded, tending them through
the fevers that followed their injuries, writing letters home
for those who were not able to write, even teaching some
of them how to draw and paint as recovery slowly came.
The worst job was carrying away the shattered arms and
legs the surgeons had amputated.

"Distant gunfire," Burkhart said again as we watched
Hurley turn the corner.

That evening I ate in the tepee. Two Songs moved
silently around, bringing good-tasting food for Burkhart
and me as we sat cross-legged on brightly colored mats.
It was exciting to be there with this man I liked and with
this beautiful Indian girl whose movements were so
graceful and whose voice, in her own tongue, was so soft
and strange, and whose few English words were so care-
ful and correct and, somehow, tender, maybe because
they were reaching across the divide set between races.
Burkhart smiled a little in the half-darkness of candle-
light, as if he understood.

11

I ran back home under the stars. In the Eldo house there was great concern. Hurley had disappeared without a goodbye or explanation. Pinned to the outhouse door, Alice had found a note:

JEST MOVD ON. A HOLE LOT
OF THANKS FUR YOR CARIN.

LOVE
HURLEY.

Chapter 4

MISSING HURLEY

We had never realized how much we would miss Hurley, because we had never thought he might go. But now he was gone, and there was a sadness when we knew he would not come in from the outhouse at breakfast time, nor be asked to stand tall for the amusement of strangers. And I felt a lonesome pang when I passed his spade, leaning against the outhouse wall. One day, I was about to move it inside, so I would not keep seeing it, but an odd superstitious feeling made me leave it untouched, as if to move it would mean bad luck that would prevent him from ever returning.

School filled most days. It was ruled over by Miss Todd. "Ruled" is the right word, because on the front of her tall desk, alongside pens and chalks, there was a yellow wooden ruler she used for pointing at the blackboard, or pointing at children, or conducting when we practiced hymns, or rapping our knuckles when we misremembered, or whacking our legs when we misbehaved. But

13

the school was really ruled over, not by Miss *Toad,* as we sometimes called her, nor by her ruler. It was ruled by the "quirt," a fearsome leather thing that lay coiled like a snake in her cupboard, four inches of braided handle for her bony hand, and twelve inches of thong for our back-sides. Whenever Miss Toad opened the cupboard door there was always fear in the class, until she simply took down a book, a rolled map, or some such welcome aid to our learning.

After school, there were a few chores like chopping firewood for Mama Eldo, or shining boots for her guests, or fetching goods from Dolly Emms's store. After Hurley disappeared, I was often glad to be busy so I would miss him less. The few boys of about the same age as myself were usually doing similar chores. At other times, we might meet for a fishing party somewhere along the creek, or sit behind buildings to tell stories or pretend to enjoy the foul mixture of various herbs we smoked in crude pipes we shaped with our knives. One afternoon, a few weeks after Hurley left, I felt awful lonesome but just didn't want the usual company. I went up over the slope to the derelict cabin, even half hoping I might find Hurley had returned and was living there.

It was much as it had been on the day I hid to watch Burkhart. Hurley was not there. I sat and lit my pipe, then quickly let it go out, as there was nobody expecting me to pretend. Then I imagined back to Burkhart saying, "Come out of there." I said it aloud, sharply, sharper than Burkhart had by far, because his way of talking was what Mama Eldo called "kinda casual."

"Are you coming out of there?" I gave myself the same scare I had felt on that day, spying. Then I waited, as I had before, down on one knee. Then I said it again, trying Burkhart's voice. Then I stood and slowly went out, and walked down the slope, as if Burkhart was there drawing Two Songs sitting on the white horse. I stood a while, imagining. But now the shadows were darker than on that day. When Two Songs put on her dress and jumped down, she was more hidden, but she smiled as before, and my voice said, "Your wife is beautiful," and Burkhart's said, "She is also modest, and you must go."

I climbed back up the slope. Going down the other side, I was the horse, cantering, carrying Burkhart and his bride over the hill. Smoke was rising from the little settlement as fires were kindled for cooking, and the waters of the creek were a darkening gold in the low sunlight.

Before going home, I went to Burkhart. "You said you would teach me to draw."

"I've been waiting for you to ask," he said.

Chapter 5

THE TRIBE THAT DISAPPEARED

"**W**hy are you called Cappy?"

It was the next day. Burkhart was painting a picture of me as we sat in his cabin. I was trying to draw the curved clay pot in which he kept his paintbrushes. The difficult part was to make both sides of it have the same shape. Burkhart had begun by drawing the left side for me. Then he asked me to draw the right to match. Now I was drawing the whole pot, over and over, getting better and better, he said. As we talked, it was not possible to tell what he was thinking. His face stayed the same, his eyes looking intently at me, then going to his picture on the easel.

"My father had a cap. I can't remember, but Bessie told me. He used to put it on me, and his pipe in my mouth. Then I used to get it and put it on myself. It was miles too big, and everyone smiled. Bessie said I must have liked them smiling, so I wore it more and more, and everyone started calling me Cappy. He brought it from England."

"Have you still got it?"

"It's still around somewhere."

"Find it. I'll make a picture of you in it." He paused in his painting. "Show me your drawing."

"It ain't easy," I said, but I saw he was pleased.

"Most worthwhile things aren't."

"I'd like to draw horses."

"You will."

I wanted to believe him. He guessed my doubts.

"It won't be *easy*, but one day you'll be able to draw anything."

One day, I thought, I'd like to be able to draw Two Songs sitting on her pony. One day seemed a long way off, but I carried on drawing the brush pot with a strange feeling of excitement. We worked in silence, but when Burkhart spoke again it seemed that my thoughts of Two Songs had somehow come into his own head.

Then he told me about the Mandans. They were a small tribe that lived further north, near the Canadian border. A tribe much liked by the white trappers and traders who passed through their territory. A tribe of fear-less huntsmen and warriors, and beautiful women. But, unlike many tribes, the Mandans preferred a life of peace and contentment, growing crops, playing games, living in permanent homes, not always moving on. Of course, they had enemies, mainly the Sioux, who raided their villages and were fought off with fierce bravery. Then came the smallpox disease.

It was brought up by the Missouri River by steamboat travelers. Because the Indians had never encountered it before the white man came, their bodies had no resistance. And it was more deadly to the Mandans than to any others, because of the way they lived close together, behind wooden fences that kept out the Sioux. The lodges they lived in, built more like houses than tepees or wigwams, sometimes contained whole families—uncles, aunts, cousins, grandparents—as many as forty or fifty people. So the smallpox spread quickly.

It made bodies swell up, and the victims died within three hours. They would plunge into the river to get relief from the heat of the fever, but there was no relief. Some drowned. Some stabbed knives into their hearts. One old chief watched helplessly as his whole family died. Only he was left, with his loved ones strewn around him. In his misery he went out and sat on a hill to starve himself to death. After six days he stumbled back to his lodge, lay down with his family, and in three more days he died.

All that was thirty years ago, when Two Songs's

mother was a child. She had been one of a small number of survivors, found when a party from the Arikara tribe had raided the Mandan village sometime later. They were taken as slaves. The lives of the adults were made so miserable that when the Arikara were attacked by the Sioux, the Mandans ran toward the attackers, shouting insults deliberately, to get themselves killed. So ended the Mandan people, except for a few children. And one of these was the girl who would become mother of Two Songs.

When Burkhart had finished the story, the afternoon shadows were falling through the window. He had stopped painting. I had forgotten my drawing. Two Songs came in with food and drink and clapped her hands with delight when she saw our work. I knew that one day I would be an artist like Burkhart, maybe even have a beautiful Indian wife. But that was far, far ahead, in a future I could not begin to imagine. And, on that lovely afternoon of work and friendship, I certainly could not have believed in the terrible event that was soon to happen.

Chapter 6

AN INDIAN'S ARROW

I found my cap in the bottom of Bessie's cupboard. It now fit somewhat better. The soft part was still too big, simply because it had been made that way, in some fashion of long ago. But the peak now stayed above my eyes, even if only just above them. I looked in the mirror and played with different ways of wearing the odd thing. When I had settled for a high tilt backwards and a bit to the right, I went downstairs, ready to visit Burkhart, really quite pleased with how I looked. I wondered how my father had worn it. It seemed to sit just right the way I had it, as if he had worn it that way too. This thought gave me a feeling of knowing him a little.

"Heavens," said Alice. "I hain't seen that for ages." She stood in front of me, blocking the way to the yard door. "Here, let me—" She pulled the peak down a little. "Not so high, but a bit more to the side." She stood back, pleased. "That's how. Keep it like that."

There was the stink of perfume on her. She thought it

was good, but it was awful, a bottle Bessie had given her, bought from a traveling salesman. But I liked her touching my cheek when she pulled my cap down, because there was nobody looking on.

"Maybe," I said.

"You should keep wearin' it," Alice said.

I went to Burkhart. He was sitting on a box outside the tepee, making a drawing of Two Songs as she stretched out on the grass. He put down his drawing to welcome me, and Two Songs sat up.

"Ah, the cap. It suits you," Burkhart said.

Two Songs sprang to her feet. She came to me and touched the cap, a hand on each side of my face. She said something I could not understand, smiling.

"She would like to try it on," said Burkhart.

"Yes." I nodded, and she understood.

I let her take it off, and she stood smiling, holding the cap up between us, then put it on. She stood with her hands still raised, a few inches away from her ears, with an expectant look, wanting us to say something.

I said yes, not knowing what else she would understand.

Burkhart took up his sketchbook and said something to her. She dropped her arms, linked a few fingers together in front of her lap, and stood looking at him shyly, perfectly still, while he drew her. Slowly, trying not to be noticed, I dropped to the grass and watched, looking now at Burkhart, now at Two Songs, until the drawing was finished.

Burkhart put the sketchbook, open, on the box, and stretched on his back. Two Songs sat beside him. I looked at the drawing. It showed her just as she had stood there. I could hardly believe that a drawing could look so true.

Two Songs held out a hand. I took up the book and gave it to her. She looked at her picture for a while, silently, in delight.

"Cappy Two Songs," she said.

While Two Songs prepared their food, Burkhart had me sit on the ground and made a drawing of me, with the cap on. It was on the same page as the drawing of Two Songs, so it appeared that I was sitting near her feet. I liked it, and so did Burkhart, and when Two Songs came out she clapped her hands with pleasure. She said something to Burkhart, questioning. He obviously agreed, and he carefully tore out the page and handed it to her. She came to me, holding it out.

"You, Cappy. You have."

While Two Songs went back to her cooking, I went with Burkhart up the pasture behind the cabin to feed and water the horses. As we walked back, there was smoke rising from all over the settlement, with the good smell of cooking on the air. Burkhart put an arm across my shoulder. "What could be more perfect than life is here in Buffalo Sky?"

"I love the drawing," I said.

I collected it and turned to go as Burkhart went into the tepee, dragging in the box on which he had sat.

An Indian with a bow in his hand was walking down the road toward me. He was very upright. His moccasins made no sound in the soft earth. His face was bony, his eyes deep and dark. He glanced down at me without turning his head. Past, he suddenly raised the bow and fixed an arrow. He swung slightly to the left, and the bow twanged. The arrow ripped through the hide of the tepee. Another twang. Another arrow.

Now the Indian was running, and in a moment he had disappeared.

Burkhart did not come out. I ran to the tepee and through the opening. Burkhart was lying over the box. An arrow was deep in his back. Blood was spreading across his shirt. I cried out, but he didn't know. I lifted his head, and blood ran out of his mouth. My hands shook. I let his head down. His chest made a noise like a dog whining. He didn't know I had lifted his head. He didn't know. He was dead. He was dead. Don't let it be true. Please don't let it be true.

And Two Songs came screaming, screaming.

Chapter 7

A LONG WAY OFF

Miss Toad told me to stop blubbering.

I said, "I ain't blubberin'."

"What, then, is the noise you're making?"

"I ain't makin' no noise."

"No noise?" She held up a hand for silence. "Can the class hear no noise? Class, listen."

I tried desperately to choke my breath, to let no sound escape, but a small sob came up from inside and broke out between my teeth. Someone in the class gave a squeaky laugh. Miss Toad picked up her ruler.

I could choke my feelings back no more. I was gasping, spluttering, and making odd little wailing noises. Miss Toad must have decided to wait. Through the blur, I could see faces turned to watch me.

"I think I was not far off, Cappy Carew." I heard her stupid voice, and suddenly, instead of blubbering, something else leaped inside me, and nothing in the world mattered as much as letting it leap out.

"You were a long way off," I shouted. "You were a long way off, you silly old fool!"

I was standing, walking toward her, turning at the front of the class, going toward the door.

"Sit down," she screeched.

"You were a long way off," I shouted. "And I'm goin' off! And I'm never comin' back!"

Miss Toad rushed at me with her ruler raised. I saw the scared, excited faces of children. She slashed the ruler at my legs, and I grabbed it from her. I put one end of it on the floor and stamped my boot in the middle. It snapped, and I waved the piece in my hand and flung it across the room.

"You'll not go out of that door," she screeched.

"Watch me," I shouted. I opened the door and saw the sunlight on the hillside through the window in the dark little porch. I slammed the door behind me, then opened it again. "Watch me," I shouted, and shut the door for the last time.

I walked across the hill a short way and sat down. The school looked as if there might be nobody in it, but I knew it was a little wooden prison in which we all spent too many hours of too many days, obeying the commands of Toad.

"Toad," I called. I started to laugh, and called "Toad" again. My blubbering for the man who had been buried yesterday was gone, and though I felt it should not have gone, and though I knew it would come back, I laughed and laughed, and called "Toad" over and over, until my throat was hoarse.

I wondered if anyone could hear, and, for some reason I did not know, I wished Hurley could hear. Where was he? Why had he gone? I wanted to tell him about Burkhart.

Then I was aware of Miss Toad's face at a window. I knew she would have to be standing on a desk, because the windows were too high for her as well as for the rest of us. She looked out for a while, then disappeared. I waited to see if she might come out of the porch doorway, ready to move off if she did. But the door stayed closed for the next half hour. When it opened, Alice came out.

EMBARRASSED

I stood in the porch doorway for a moment, then walked across the hill toward Cappy. I knew he would be think- ing I had been sent by Miss Toad to persuade him to come in. He put one hand up to his eyes, and I thought he could be crying, but as I came nearer I could see he was making a spy-hole with his curled fingers to watch me through. When I was close, he fixed on my face.

"Why are you doing that?"

"No reason."

"Then don't," I said. "It's embarrassin'."

"Why you embarrassed?"

"Lookin' at me."

"Nothin' wrong with that."

"I just don't like it. I like to see where you're lookin'."

"You can see I'm lookin' at your face."

"You are now, but . . . it just ain't nice." I dropped to my knees and grasped his fist. "So—"

He let his hand be pulled away. I realized that it had been there to hide him from the embarrassment of facing me after what he had done in the classroom. And he knew that I knew.

"Don't be bothered," I said.

"I ain't bothered."

I knew he would say that.

"You don't have to be, not with me," I said.

He was looking at me. I wondered if he was thinking I was pretty. It seemed like he had never seen me before. I guess he had always thought of me as good and plain and ordinary. But he was looking at me like I was pretty.

"Why'd you come out?" he said.

"I offered to come and tell you come back in." As I said it, I felt kind of teasing.

"Well, I ain't comin'!"

"I know that."

"Why'd you come, then?"

"To get out. I ain't goin' back either."

Chapter 9

An Unwelcome Visitor

We waited in the outhouse.

"Look, I can't go back after what I done," Cappy said. "Not in a hundred years."

"I guess not." I thought of his face as he flung the piece of broken ruler across the schoolroom.

"But you could go. Make excuse you stayed out tryin' to persuade me."

"No," I said. "I'm finished there."

We were sitting on Hurley's bed in the gloomy corner at the side of the copper tub. We had heard my sister Henny come through the yard to the kitchen door. She had started telling about what happened at school even before the door closed.

"Now they'll be ready for us," Cappy said. "I ain't too sure what we say."

"We say what happened."

"They already know. Henny had to go tellin'." Cappy

was riled up. "I wasn't blubberin', anyway. Toad was just pickin' on me."

"She was. Anyone could tell," I said.

"Not what I'd call blubberin'."

"No, you wasn't," I said. It was the right thing to say.

"Old bitch don't know what ain't blubberin' is," Cappy said.

"Old bitch," I said.

We fell back on Hurley's bed and kind of laughed a bit, then were quiet, listening, because the latch of the gate clicked again. There were footsteps, then a tap on the kitchen door.

"Miss Todd," said Mama. "You'd better come in."

The door closed. Cappy was on his feet.

"That sly old—" He didn't know which word to use. He was going to say "bitch" again, but that was the word that had made us laugh, and now we weren't laughing.

I still sat on the bed. Cappy was at the window.

"Best I go in," I said. "See what she's sayin'."

"I stay here. Best I don't show."

"Yes, you stay here." I was at the door. "I'll come back when she's gone." In spite of being nervous, a funny thought struck me. I had a picture in my head of Cappy coming in and stamping on Miss Toad's umbrella, which she always carried. Cappy saw me smile.

"Ain't funny," he said. When I looked back from the kitchen door, his face was at the outhouse window.

I went straight through into the parlor. Bessie and Miss Todd were sitting, and Mama had just set down a tea tray.

"Well," said Mama. "Well, well, well . . ."

I stood waiting. Mama was pouring tea, with her back to me. Bessie moved a little table for Miss Todd to set her cup on, and handed her a cup of tea.

"Very kind," said Miss Todd.

Mama sat and looked at me.

"You'd better sit down, Miss," she said. Her voice sounded like trouble. "Miss Todd has not just come to take afternoon tea."

I sat on the piano stool, so I was not too close to them.

"I know," I said.

"Well, you'd better say something."

"Cappy was upset about Mister Burkhart . . ." I began.

"I mean say something about yourself," said Mama.

"When I went to Cappy on the hill, he was too upset to come back into school."

"So you stayed out yourself," said Miss Todd.

"Yes, he needed me to talk to."

"Where's Cappy now?" asked Bessie.

"He wouldn't want me to say."

"Bessie has asked you a question," said Mama.

When I still hesitated, Bessie said, "She don't have to say." I thought that was right understanding, just like Bessie always was.

I said, "Thank you." Miss Todd's throat went up and down, a bit like a toad's, but she said nothing out loud.

"Well, if you think so, Bessie," Mama said.

"Are we thinking of Cappy's own good?" asked Miss Todd. "It does a boy no good to go beyond himself, as he did. They have to be brought back down somehow."

"Back *down?*" said Bessie.

"That moment when he broke the ruler and flung it across the schoolroom." She half-stood up to fling out her hand to show us Cappy's action. "Then stamped out and slammed the door!" She sat down, angry. "'Watch me,' he shouted, and he opened the door and jeered at me. 'Watch me,' he shouted again. He needs to be brought down from that."

"I apologize for him," said Bessie quietly, "and he will apologize for himself later."

"And said he was never coming back," said Miss Todd, calming.

"We shall have to see about that," said Bessie.

"Alice will talk him into changing his mind," said Mama.

I thought, No Alice won't.

Bessie was sipping her tea. "Where was the ruler?" she asked Miss Todd.

"He flung one piece right across the room to the window."

"I mean, *before he broke it.*"

"He jumped at me and snatched it. Snatched it, and broke it under his boot."

"He has been very upset by the killing of Mister Burkhart," said Mama. "That man had become a great friend and teacher to Cappy."

"Do you mean you were *hitting* him with it?" Bessie asked.

"I had not hit him."

"Because he didn't give you the chance, Miss Todd." Bessie seemed angry. "I understand. I understand very well. I grew up in a hard school myself. Not a school building, Miss Todd. I mean the world. The world I grew up in was a hard school. But it gave me a soft heart. I'm not Cappy's mother, but I know when a bit of understandin' is the thing that's needed. And I'll give it. And when he needs someone in the world to lean on, I'm here for him. And cold creatures like you needn't expect no help from me to bring a good boy down."

"I've heard of your reputation as a giver of comfort," Miss Todd said.

Mama stood up. "Will you have more tea, Miss Todd? I think you were not intending that remark to be a slur."

"I think I mean I must be on my way," said Miss Todd. She stood. "Thank you for the tea, ma'am."

When she had gone, Mama and Bessie looked at each other and smiled. When their backs were turned, I went to the outhouse. Cappy was not there.

Chapter 10

THUD, THUD, THUD

After a minute of waiting in the outhouse, I was too edgy to stay. I crept out, went down the path at the back of the settlement, and came to the pasture behind Burkhart's cabin. The white horse and the pony were there grazing, and I watched them for a while, full of sad thoughts, and spoke to them a bit about Burkhart, and told them he was okay somewhere. They both came and nuzzled up, and it was good to be with them. Then I went down to the cabin to see Two Songs.

She had been crying, and not caring for herself. Her hair was loosened and hung around her shoulders. The strings of beads she always wore were thrown on the floor. She had been taking the paintings off the wall. They were in neat sets at the end of the room, tied together with cords. When I came to the door, which was open, letting the afternoon sunlight in, she was holding one of Burkhart's pictures of himself. She held it up for me to see, and said something I could not understand. She shook her head gently and smiled a bit.

"Good Cappy."

She put the picture by the wall. For a moment she put a hand on each of my shoulders and just looked at me, then slid them behind my neck and held me close. Her heart was going thud, thud, thud in my ear, thud, thud, thud, thud . . .

When she let me go, there was something she wanted to tell me, but I could understand nothing of what she said. So she took one of Burkhart's sketchbooks and began to make a pencil drawing. It was small and sharp, and very simple, with a tepee, an arrow going through a hole, the Indian with a bow. She pointed to the Indian's face, then made a quick drawing, a bit larger, of the face alone, showing the dark eyes, the bony cheeks, which were fixed in my mind and had been in my dreams every night. She said a name, then, making shadows of her fingers fall at different lengths across the page, she made me understand the meaning, and when I said, "Long Shadow," she put a long shadow behind the figure with the bow.

Then she drew the front wall of the cabin, with an arrow going through the window, others sticking into the logs, others falling on the roof, flaming, with scribbles of smoke. She pointed to herself, and grasped both hands at the air, showing herself being seized. She meant that she was afraid he would try to burn the cabin and take her away. The drawings went in a row across the page, like writing in pictures instead of words. There was Burkhart on his horse. Then she put herself sitting behind him, and she wiped a tear on her sleeve. Reaching the edge of the page, she started another row of pictures below, with Long Shadow reaching out to her as she turned her face away from him. Maybe she meant to show he had wanted her, but she had gone away with Burkhart.

As she made the drawings, she talked. Sometimes I could understand the meaning of a word and tried to show that I understood by saying the English word. Sometimes she showed that she recognized what I said. Soon the page was covered. In one picture, Two Songs was Long Shadow's squaw, lying in his tepee. It was what he saw in his imagination. At the bottom corner of the page, he was outside the Sioux encampment, turned away, as if he no longer belonged among the many tepees. I could not tell whether he had chosen to leave his people or had been banished.

By the time Two Songs handed me the sketchbook, she was ready to pick up her beads from the floor. She began to comb her hair. I looked at the story in the pictures. The one of Long Shadow coming to her in the te-pee was kind of rude, but she did not seem to know, though she had smiled as she made it.

The sun was lower, coming further into the room. Suddenly, Alice was in the doorway. Two Songs sprang up in welcome. Momentarily, against the light, I thought I saw Burkhart standing by the white horse in the pasture. Later, I told Bessie. She said, "We have to be able to be-lieve things like that."

Chapter 11

A SPECIAL GUEST

There was a tapping on the kitchen door in the middle of the night. Mama Eldo and Bessie were just on their way to bed after sitting up to play cards with two guests from back East, who had come off the stagecoach that afternoon. When Bessie opened the door, Two Songs stood there in terror, trying to tell what had happened. Mama Eldo took her in and sat her in the kitchen, while Bessie came and woke me because Two Songs was asking for me. Because of things she had said when she made the drawings, I was able to understand something of what she was now saying. Long Shadow had come back and put two flaming arrows into a wall of the cabin, on either side of a window. Then he had put his face to the window, lit by the flames. He had told her to come with him. She had refused, and he had said he would come back another day with other Indians, to carry her off. Before he went, he had put out the flames, which had been meant only to frighten her. She had run along the back path to our house.

Mama Eldo heated milk for us all, and we went to bed. Two Songs was given blankets, and she made herself comfortable on the parlor floor in front of the dwindling fire. For a while, I could not get back to sleep. There was a low sound of voices from Bessie's room. I opened the door of my wall cupboard so I might listen to what they were saying. I recognized the voice of one of the men from back East, but could not hear distinct words. I went back to bed, and was soon asleep.

In the morning, Mama Eldo insisted that Two Songs should come to live with us for a time. Two Songs seemed nervous, but pleased to be safe. So, with help of the two guests, we all carried her possessions from the cabin and stored most of them in the outhouse. Two Songs made it clear that she was happy to sleep on the floor, so a mattress was put between the sisters' beds. Henny had gone to school, but neither Mama Eldo nor Bessie mentioned the fact that Alice and I had stayed away.

"They think we've stayed home to help with this," said Alice. "Just wait till afternoon."

But in the afternoon we all helped Two Songs take down the tepee and carry it up to the house, and still school was not mentioned.

★
★ ★

Chapter 12

LIKE A LITTLE DOG

Two Songs liked living with us. She was very sad some-times, and would want to go in the outhouse and sit among the things that had belonged to Mr. Burkhart. One day, Bessie said I should ask Mama if we could take down some of the pictures in the house and put up some of Mr. Burkhart's paintings instead. So Two Songs and I spent a happy afternoon taking down some of the dull old things, like *Queen Victoria* of England, and *George Washington at Valley Forge,* given by guests, Mama said, to lighten their baggage. Then we went in the outhouse, and Two Songs chose some of the paintings she liked most. They had never been framed, but there was a bag of hooks among Mr. Burkhart's equipment, so we fixed hooks and cords, and when we had finished, near bed-time, the house looked like a picture gallery, one of the guests said. Everyone came with us from room to room, inspecting by lamplight, and we were up early in the morning to see how our gallery looked in the light of day.

"I bet there ain't a better artist in America," Cappy said.

A guest from Boston said, "I think you may not be exaggerating." He patted Cappy's shoulder. "You may not be exaggerating."

I looked at Cappy, expecting him to be grinning with pleasure, but a huge tear came in his eye as he turned away.

Later, when we were alone, I told him something. "I cried like mad in bed last night."

"Why?"

"Just sad."

"I know," he said.

"So many pictures, and now he can't see them."

We did not know what to do about sadness. It came sometimes when we didn't expect it, and it didn't go away just because we told it to go. Sometimes, I wanted to run out somewhere, and run and run until I had run all the sadness out of me.

But I didn't even start most times, because it wouldn't work, or, if it did, the same feeling would come back until I had let it get at me till it was satisfied.

"Sad again?" Bessie asked me one day. I nodded. "Sadness is like a little dog pulling at our skirts," she said. "It just won't be shaken off."

"It's a big dog," I said.

"You should be back at school, maybe. Maybe it ain't the best place in the world, but it's somewhere to be busy and take your mind off bein' sad."

We had been through all the expected trouble about refusing to go back to school.

"You're both around the age for leavin'," Mama said. "If it was Henny, I'd slap her bottom and tell her do as she's told, but you're too big for that."

"What age did you leave, Mama?"

"About the same. But it was different then. Not everyone even got the chance of goin' to school."

"I was twelve," Bessie said. "But I might have turned out better if I'd been able to stay on."

I wasn't sure what turning out better could mean. Bessie seemed good enough to me. There were other discussions about what Cappy and I should do, and whether we might find work to do that would bring us wages. But both Mama and Bessie were content not to hurry us. Henny told me that Mama had said maybe I might want to go back to school if Miss Todd would promise not to "make an example" of me.

"What does that mean?" Henny asked.

"Whip my ass, maybe."

"Stand you in the corner."

"Pull my hair."

We laughed, and suddenly I felt like I was closer to Henny than I had begun to think I was.

One afternoon, when the house was quiet, I stood and looked at myself in the long mirror on Mama's wardrobe.

Gettin' titties ain't everything, I thought. No, but it was something, and I would never be like Henny again.

Chapter 13

FLAMES IN THE NIGHT

I was having bad dreams. I kept on seeing the face of the Indian at the window, lit by flaming arrows. But now it was not at Burkhart's cabin, as Two Songs had seen it on her night of terror. It was at my own bedroom window, and I woke up in a sweat, shouting.

One night, Bessie heard me and came in to see what was wrong. She sat on the bed and talked about how daft our minds could be, as well as clever, and said most people's minds were more daft than clever, and everybody had ghastly fears, even when they pretended they didn't.

A few nights after that, when the dream had come again, I got out of bed and went to look from the window. The curtains were closed. I knew there would be no face, so I opened them boldly. Moonlight streamed in. It was making everywhere a strange whitish color, like snow at night, though it was in the middle of summer. The school roof shone, but the nearside wall stood dark against it. As I stood looking at the hill, I remembered Burkhart and Two Songs on the cantering white horse, and longed for them to be riding there now. I was pulling the curtains together again when I noticed a figure on the top of the hill. Somehow, I knew instantly that it was Long Shadow. He ran across toward the school, stood in its shadow for a moment, then moved down to the nearer buildings of the settlement away to the left, the little church and a barn, where I could no longer see him.

I was wide awake, and my heart was racing. I grabbed my pants and started to dress. It would be impossible to go calmly back to bed. There was no point in waking Mama Eldo or Bessie. If Hurley had still been down in the outhouse, I would have gone to him, and he would have known what was best to do. He would most likely have said we should see where the Indian was going, but keep our distance.

I crept down the stairs and let myself out silently, deciding to go by the back path to Burkhart's cabin. As I came down from the back pasture, I kept under the shadow of the trees and bushes, and just as I was nearing the cabin from one end, Long Shadow appeared at the other. I stood absolutely still, except that I was shivering.

Long Shadow stood looking at the front of the cabin, as if he sensed that something was different. Did he know that Two Songs was not there? He was standing in full moonlight, his bow in his hand. Would there be more flaming arrows? Should I dare to make a noise to alarm him? Would he run, knowing he would have his chance some other night? More likely, I thought, he would send an arrow in the direction of the noise.

As I watched, he went up to the cabin and tried to peer through a narrow gap in the shutters. Then he went around the building, trying each shutter.

I ducked low in the shadows. At the back, very near to me, he took one of the branches Burkhart had trimmed ready for sawing for firewood, and leaned it against the cabin. Then he took a second branch and placed it about a foot away from the other. With a hand and foot on each, he shinned up, caught the edge of the roof timbers, and swung himself onto the roof.

He stood clear in the moonlight, tall and upright, as he had been on the day he killed Burkhart. His bony cheeks caught the light. The caves of his eyes were so dark that I could not tell if he could see me. Then I knew I was safe, because he turned away.

I couldn't see what he did, but there was a flare of matchlight near a chimney. He moved quickly across the roof and jumped down. He stood with his back to me, so close that I could almost have touched him. He stepped back even closer, and at that instant an explosion came. Glass broke, shutters flew open. Smoke came from the windows. Then flames were leaping.

Now Long Shadow ran. He went up the pasture and disappeared. I ran past the cabin and into the road. I shouted, "Fire," but already faces were at windows, and two men ran with buckets. I stood where the tepee had been, trembling.

The fire took hold. The cabin was filled with crackling, creaking, and banging. Men shouted, women screamed. Burkhart's home became a place of flames. Brighter and brighter, higher and higher, under the white moon.

Chapter 14

THE WICKER CHAIR

After the cabin burned down, Cappy was changed. When he was in the house, he didn't want to talk much.

The day after the fire, we went down with Two Songs and looked at the patch of ashes, which was all that was left, with two iron stoves standing in the midst, burned to a dull red. It was so sad, Mama and Bessie were crying as they hugged Two Songs. When she pulled away, she stooped and put a finger in the ash and touched a gray spot on her forehead.

Cappy kicked through the ashes, then stood in one place awhile, just looking down.

"That was where I sat drawing with him," he said afterward.

"You were drawing?"

"Yeah."

"I didn't know that."

"You don't know everything," he said, like he was bad

tempered. I knew it was his mood, and let it go.

From then, he started to draw again. He borrowed a clay pot that Mr. Burkhart's brushes were in, and sat in the parlor, drawing it through a whole afternoon, while Two Songs and I helped Mama and Bessie baking in the kitchen. When we went into the parlor, he had just finished, and the drawing was marvelous.

"I didn't know you could draw like that," said Mama.

"I can't," said Cappy.

That seemed a strange thing to say, for there the drawing was.

"Sometimes we can do things," Bessie said, "and don't know how."

"I'm just workin' at it," Cappy said.

Next day, when we were alone, I said, "Draw me."

"I can't."

"Just for practice. It don't have to be good."

"You sit still for ages?"

"I can try."

"Come in my room."

I went in his bedroom, which was against Mama's rules. He said I should sit in the wicker chair, looking out of the window. Like that, he wouldn't have to draw the whole of my face, because he wasn't up to doing that just yet. So he did a drawing of me, part from behind, just catching the side of my cheek and the fall of my hair, and my shoulder and arm, against the window, and it took an hour to do, not counting the rests we had, and it was truly good for a first-ever try, and I loved it.

Mr. Burkhart had given him a sketchbook. He wouldn't show me what else was in it.

"You draw me again sometime?"

"Mama must change her rule about bedrooms," Cappy said.

Chapter 15

FORBIDDEN

There was a place on the creek where we were forbidden to go. It was beyond where the boys fished, hidden from the settlement by trees at a bend in the creek, at the foot of the hill below the derelict cabin. It was a pool formed by rock, and it was a forbidden place because, many years ago, two children bathing there had been carried off by Indians, and were never seen again. We were not sure the story was true.

Older children went there to bathe. Boys and girls went separately. It was our own strict rule. And even though the girls always took two boys to be sentries on the rocks, to warn in case of danger, they never saw the bathing, and the rule was never broken. There was a story that, long ago, a boy on sentry watch had spied on bathers, and the angry girls had hurled him from the top of the rock. When his drowned body was found, there was an image of the girl who had pushed him, fixed and

clear, in his dead eyes. His name was George Washington
Xavier, and he was the son of a French fur trapper. The
girl's name was Blanche. We did not know that the story
was any truer than the other story. But the rule was
never, never broken again, it was said.

I was not so sure. It seemed natural that, once in a
while, one of the sentries might have a big load of curiosity that just had to be satisfied. The thought of that never
bothered me much. He would never tell, would he? How
he slithered up the rock like a snake, just far enough to
put his forehead and eyes up to take a peek, then slithered down again. He would never tell that, would he,
with the thought of them dead eyes and Blanche's picture fixed in them?

Soon after she came to live with us, I took Two
Songs. We met three girls and spent an hour at swimming and laughing together. Two Songs made us all
amazed and envious. In the water, she was like a shad-
owy fish, gliding far down, turning, rising a bit and gliding
some more, just under the surface. She would shoot up
into the air with gasps and cries of fun, then flip over and
go down again, her feet pointing up in a gleam then
gone. On the bank, she was modest and silent. She
stayed on the far side, so we only saw her from a way off.
She was uncommon beautiful. If one of us went too near,

she slipped into the pool with a laugh and glided away.

As we walked home, the two sentries were walking behind. We stopped to pay them. It was the custom for each girl to give a cent or some small present. Sometimes, the cheeky ones gave a kiss into the bargain, but that was only for the kind of boy who would like it. Most boys would shy away from that. It seemed like a little coin was better than a dozen kisses. But on this day it was plain that one of them would have loved dearly to have a kiss from Two Songs. She had no money to give, so I paid him double and said it was from her, and gave him a look like I knew his secret.

He was kind of shamed, and said something about "squaw" behind us. The girls were quiet and giggly by turns. They tried to talk to Two Songs. One asked her if she was going back to her own people. Two Songs didn't understand. I told them, "One day, maybe."

In the evening, I was telling Two Songs some English words. She was saying "swim" and "deep" and "rock" and other words that came from the afternoon. Then she tried to tell me something that needed too many of her own words, so she took a sketchbock and pencil and made a drawing. There was a pool, not the one of the afternoon but one she knew somewhere else, with steep rocks all around. In the water were many bathing women and children, tiny figures that made her smile as she drew them, and on the rock tops were sentries with bows and muskets, all facing away to keep the bathers safe.

I asked her to draw herself in that place. She drew a child, and meant that for a joke. I told her to draw herself as she was now. It amused her to show herself facing away, head and shoulders, her hair floating out. She looked at my face and laughed.

She put the drawing aside and started to undress for sleep. I went to the kitchen to fetch hot milk. Henny was listening with Mama and Bessie to Cappy telling of digging a latrine. She went ahead of me to bed and was asleep by the time I brought in milk for Two Songs. Two Songs was sleepy too. She roused enough to drink, then turned over. Her hair, spread behind her over the coverlet, reminded me of her hair floating out on the water. As I brought the candle to the bedside table, I noticed the sketchbook propped at the side of her pillow so I would see it as I lay in bed. There was a little drawing of herself just below the other two.

"You like?" she asked.

"Yes . . . I like."

As I sat on the edge of my bed, she moved aside, to make a space. I took it and fit against her, and fell asleep without a word.

Chapter 16

DIGGING

There was a bell on the back of the door. It jangled loudly to call Dolly Emms through from her kitchen, but she was already at the counter.

"Master Cappy?" she said. "What can I do for you?"

"I'm doin' Hurley's work. You wanted some diggin'."

"Ah, my latrine. Oh, yes, I do want some digging. What would be your charge?"

I hadn't thought of the charge. I felt stupid.

"Nothin'. I'll just do it for Hurley."

"Well, you can't do it for nothing. I won't have that. Business is business. Come out back. I'll show you what you have to do, and when you've done it as well as Hurley would . . . well, I'll pay you what I would have paid him, poor man."

I followed her through a passage out to the backyard, where there was mainly rough grass, with a path leading to a privy.

On the hillside, beyond the valley of the creek, were half a dozen Indians on horseback, riding at walking pace downward to the right. I wondered if they might be the Sioux Long Shadow had said he would bring to carry off Two Songs. I said nothing to Dolly Emms, but kept my eye on them.

"Five feet long, at least four deep, and two feet wide," she was saying.

The doorbell jangled. She hurried off. I started to dig. The Indians circled, then lined up and had a race, letting out yells as they went. They turned at a wiry tree on the far left and galloped back. They circled again, then watched each other do the trick of sliding off the horse's back and hanging along its side. Two went right under the belly and came up on the other side.

The ground was soft. Hurley's spade was sharp and not too heavy, but my hands were tender. I soon began to get blisters. Dolly Emms brought me a mug of tea and two jam tarts, and when she saw my hands she fetched a pair of gloves.

The Indians went away over the hill, where it dipped in the middle. Maybe I had been alarmed for no good reason. They were simply having fun.

I worked for another hour. Dolly came to say it was six o'clock and she was closing the store. She said she would expect me back in the morning. I said I would be there.

Going up the road, with the spade on my shoulder, I tried out what it was like to be Hurley, giving my crooked leg a good swing, "poor fella with the leg." And there was the memory of his voice: "They git disgusted with the wrong things, Mister Burkhart."

Alice and Two Songs stayed in their room the whole evening. I guessed they had been swimming. Now, they were close to each other, and I felt kind of jealous of that, and wasn't sure why. I guess I just wanted company. I tried to draw an Indian doing the trick of lying along the horse's side, but it wouldn't come right. The horse looked more like a dog. I tore the picture up.

I went and sat with a candle in the outhouse and looked through one of Burkhart's sketchbooks. There were many drawings of Two Songs. I felt like a spy, seeing things not meant for me. But then I thought that Burkhart, wherever he was now, would understand.

"It's okay, Cappy," his voice said in my head. "It's okay."

Straightway after breakfast, I was ready for work. I had put Hurley's spade back in its place against the outhouse wall, not just *near* its place, but exactly where Hurley had left it, not a half inch off. I still had that superstitious feeling that it had to be in the right place, so he would one day come back. Like Bessie said, our minds are more daft than clever, but I wasn't taking any chances, even if I was as daft as a chicken.

Dolly Emms left me to the digging, and I had a happy morning going down deep. By noon it was deeper than she had asked for, and I was still happy to go on. As I worked, I was thinking about things with sadness in them. I wondered how well my father had known Bessie. And a picture came into my mind of a lady in a white dress, lost in long grasses of the prairie.

When I came back after dinner, Buck Riley, the carpenter, was there. He unbolted the privy walls, and we carried the scrubbed seat over to the new trench. Buck stood with his hands in his apron pockets and said I'd made a good job. We fixed the walls in place, and Buck grinned with his yellow teeth and called into Dolly's back doorway that the seat was ready for occupation.

"This man is impossible!" Dolly said when he was going. When the door had closed behind him, she said, "And your work is worth every cent of what I've put in this envelope. You'll carry on in this place where poor Hurley left off. But don't undersell yourself, Cappy, don't undersell yourself. Ask every penny of what you're worth. You won't always be a latrine digger. There's a wide world out there, you know."

As I went home I opened the envelope. There were two new dollars inside. I forgot being Hurley, and ran.

In the evening, I wanted to be with Two Songs, but she was with Alice. I watched the sunset, thinking of my father in some distant place, beyond mountains, and wondered if he ever thought back to Bessie and the small boy, years behind him.

Chapter 17

SOLDIERS COME

A few cavalry soldiers were sitting on the grass outside the back gate. Their tethered horses were grazing. There was pipe smoke drifting up, and plenty of laughter.

Cappy and Two Songs were with me, carrying stuff from the store, and we hurried on with curiosity when we saw the blue uniforms from way off. Soldiers were a rare sight in Buffalo Sky.

When we came to the gate, the laughter dropped, and faces turned to watch.

"Pretty lil' gal," said one.

"Pretty lil' squaw," said another.

"Pretty boy," said another, and there was a burst of laughter.

We already had our backs to them, going through the yard. When we reached the kitchen, we saw there were two more inside. Mama was taking an officer into the parlor. The other man followed through, but stayed like a sentry outside the partly open door.

We put the provisions on the table. Two Songs looked anxious.

"Your men like some tea?" I asked the soldier.

"We're parched, Miss. Tea would be mighty acceptable. I'm Corporal Dancy."

I told him my name and introduced Two Songs and Cappy. He assumed Cappy was my brother, so I put him right.

When all was ready, I sent Two Songs in with a tray for Mama and the officer, and Corporal Dancy asked the officer for permission to take out tea for the men. Cappy didn't seem too interested in helping. I guessed it was embarrassment at "pretty boy." Two Songs looked pleased with herself when she came out. I had heard Mama introducing her, and the officer being gracious. Mama called him "Mister Malone," but the corporal called him "Lieutenant."

Corporal Dancy said he would take out the tea to his men. He called them "boys." I said I would help. They seemed a sassy lot of men or boys, whichever they were called, but I thought I could stand that. I didn't mind overmuch being called "pretty gal." It wasn't something that happened every day.

But the soldiers were polite, with Corporal Dancy there, and I heard only one murmur of "pretty gal." The corporal had fetched a billycan, which would hold more than a teapot, and they helped themselves from that, using their tin cups. I carried out milk and sugar.

"I expected they'd give saucy talk," the corporal said as we went back in. "They're a roughish set of boys, but good hearted. They been through a lot, some of them." He grinned. "I expected a few more 'pretty gals.'"

I caught his look and smiled back. He was nice and boyish himself.

"It don't happen every day," I said.

"I would have thought it happened all the time." It sounded like he really meant it.

"Not in a little place like this," I said.

When we came into the kitchen, Cappy was listening at the parlor door. He backed off a bit, but couldn't resist edging close again, trying to see through the gap by the hinges.

Corporal Dancy stood at his place by the door again, but further forward into the kitchen, and sipped at his tea. He let Cappy keep to his place just behind his shoulder. He seemed amused to do that, and indicated to me with a finger to watch Cappy at his spying. "This could be the most perfect cup of tea I ever tasted," he said.

I said he was just being gracious. He said it was simple truth. I said he was a gentleman, anyway. I was nervous and trying not to show it. I liked him something spectacular, and was trying to think of the way Bessie might make a conversation like this go graciously and honest at the same time. Bessie was always at ease when she talked, and she had the secret of making even the shyest stranger be at ease too. I wanted to feel I was like that with Corporal Dancy.

I asked him why the soldiers had come.

"Not my business to say, Miss Alice," he said.

"Will you be stayin'?"

"I can't say. I reckon Lieutenant Malone will be sayin'."

Cappy moved away from the door. Corporal Dancy put down his cup and stood straight. Mama opened the door wider for the officer, but he bowed a bit and allowed her through first.

"We shall have a house full of gentlemen," Mama said.

"I trust you will find us so," said Lieutenant Malone.

He was tall and slim, with gray hair, but not old. Corporal Dancy followed him out. Mama went upstairs to find Bessie.

Cappy looked bothered.

"Come in the outhouse," he said. "I'll tell you somethin'."

Chapter 18

Bad News

Cappy took me in the outhouse and told me what he had heard.

The soldiers would be staying two or three days. They needed rest.

They were hunting bands of Indians who were attacking travelers and settlements.

By her kindness in having Two Songs live with us, Mama put us all in danger. Long Shadow would follow Two Songs wherever she went.

Lieutenant Malone asked if there was a man in the house.

Mama said occasional guests, but we used to have Hurley.

He said he knew the name. He asked what sort of man Hurley was.

Mama said the best sort. And he had a wounded leg from the war.

He asked if she knew which battle.

Mama said no.

"You would say he was a fine fellow?" he said.

"Odd, but fine," Mama said.

"He's a deserter," he said.

"No! Never!" Mama said.

"I assure you, ma'am. He ran away from a battle," he said. "He got his wound in a rockfall. If he hadn't been running away, it would never have happened."

Mama said he was a lovely man, everybody liked him.

"There are lovable rogues," he said.

He said if Hurley wasn't a deserter, his wound could have been properly treated. He wouldn't have been crippled.

Mama said if he hadn't run away, he might be dead.

He said if the army had caught Hurley running, he would be dead, anyway. He would have been shot as a deserter.

He said it was in his orders to hunt Hurley down and take him prisoner.

Mama asked what would happen to him.

He said prison.

Mama said the war was over.

He said that would save him from being shot.

He said he was sorry to tell all this.

Mama said he had to carry out orders.

He said it wasn't his most important order.

He said she mustn't shelter Hurley again.

She said we didn't know where he had gone.

"That's just as well," he said.

"Don't tell the young people just yet," Mama said.

He said it was her business to do that.

Chapter 19

DAYS BEFORE THE STORM

C A P P Y

The soldiers stayed three nights. When they rode away, Alice moped around the house for a week. She was sweet on Corporal Dancy.

She was always looking at him out of the corner of her eye. She would do things for him, like brush his uniform as he smartened himself at the mirror in the hallway. When she did the same out in the yard, because he was covered in horsehairs, the soldiers joked at him, and Alice's face was the color of strawberries.

Bessie was sweet on Lieutenant Malone. They talked and drank wine in her room, late. He had lived in some of the places she had lived, or his family had. I opened my wall cupboard door and heard them saying something about St. Louis.

ALICE

Corporal Dancy gave me a special wave after all the others had stopped waving, just one more raising of his hand that I knew was for me. He had been kind of sweet on me, as I was on him. I saw him looking at me out of the corner of his eye sometimes. On the day they left, he kept glancing at me at breakfast. When we were shaking hands all around, just before they mounted up, he put his other hand on top of mine. It wasn't much, not like a kiss maybe, which Lieutenant Malone gave Bessie and Mama on the back of the hand, but with everyone looking on, he couldn't do more.

"I think you're probably a bit sweet on a uniform," Bessie said. "No harm if you don't get oversweet, because soldiers are always moving on, and you have to stay behind."

CAPPY

One of the soldiers saw me with Hurley's spade. I told him about Hurley being my friend. He said it would only be by luck if they found him. Not luck for Hurley, I said. He said he didn't think Lieutenant Malone would be trying overhard to catch Hurley. I asked him why he thought that.

He said, "The Lieutenant ain't that sort of man."

GOODBYE, BUFFALO SKY

A L I C E

Corporal Dancy's name was Dan. Dan Dancy—I liked that. Dan said he got no pleasure from chasing Indians. He said the white man drove the Indians off their own land. It was not surprising that they were angry. I asked him if he knew about Long Shadow. He said not much. I told him about Burkhart and Two Songs and Long Shadow. He said perhaps Burkhart should have left Two Songs with her own people. I said she chose to be with Burkhart. She didn't want to be wife to Long Shadow. He said that was a pity from Long Shadow's point of view. Not from Two Songs's point of view, I said.

"She's a great little beauty," he said.

I said something kind of saucy, but I was nervous. "You should see her bathin'."

I told him about the Forbidden Place.

"If we were staying longer . . . ," he joked. "Or if I ever come back this way . . ."

I told him about George Washington Xavier.

"Well, it would need some thinking about," he said. His face was red. "Would it be worth the risk?"

"I'm too shy for this conversation," I said.

"So am I," he said.

C A P P Y

After the soldiers left, I kept wondering if they might

come across Hurley somewhere, just by chance, and he might not realize they were looking for him.

I tried not to think about it too much, by keeping busy. Dolly Emms was telling people that I was now doing Hurley's work, and soon, most days, I was digging myself down into the earth, or cutting back the bushes and weeds that tried to fill every ditch Hurley had ever dug. In the afternoons sometimes, when the housework was finished, Alice and Two Songs came to watch. They would sit or lie in the dry grass, teaching each other words in their two tongues, laughing and fooling. It seemed sometimes like they wanted to tease me with their prettiness, holding a buttercup under their chins to make reflections, or holding some big leaf over their heads like a sunshade, or holding up their skirts and dancing. If I got fed up with that, I kept my head down at my work, or picked up a worm and flung it their way, or let earth fly off my spade, like carelessness.

One day, I stood up from my work for a breather, and saw, only a few yards away, the face of Long Shadow. He was watching from the cover of a hazel bush. We stared at each other for a moment. There was a streak of light down one of his cheeks, and the rest of his skin merged into the greenish shadows. Alice and Two Songs didn't see him, and they were still playing. Then he was gone.

I said nothing to the girls. If Long Shadow had

wanted to harm us then, he could have done. I couldn't understand why he had not. That evening, I found Burkhart's derringer pistol and a box of bullets in the outhouse. The derringer was small enough to go in the pocket of my pants, and I decided to carry it. I said nothing to anybody about seeing Long Shadow.

A L I C E

I missed Dan. I knew Bessie was right about not getting too sweet on soldiers. I tried not to miss him, but I couldn't help it. Then, I thought what it must be like for Two Songs, missing Burkhart. She was still real sad some days, and she sat by his grave. Sometimes she was able to forget for a while. She loved to work in the house. She was a truly good cook, and Mama allowed her to make some meals, even for guests.

I was teaching her more English words. She wanted to learn, and suddenly it seemed like she was remembering things Burkhart had said. She understood better now because she was hearing English all the time. But she wanted to speak in her own tongue too, and she started to make me say Sioux words. Cappy said she was as bad as Toad, the way she made me repeat and repeat.

While the soldiers were with us, we had seen how Lieutenant Malone had been able to speak to her a little.

Now, she told me something he had said. It was that she should go back to her own people. But Cappy told me the story Burkhart had told him, about who her people really were, not the Sioux but the Mandans.

I asked her about the Mandans. Her eyes filled with tears. "No man, no woman," she said. "No boy, no girl."

CAPPY

Old Ebenezer Riley asked me to dig his grave. I didn't know straightway what to say. He laughed, and coughed a bit with his pipe smoke, and said he knew he wasn't dead, but he thought he soon might be. I said I guessed he'd live a long while yet. He laughed again, so I joined in with the joke and asked him what he would die of. He said old age and baccy. He said he didn't mind dying of them, because you have to die of something. He said that one day soon he would take me to the graveyard and show me where he wanted to lie. Then he told me to go in Buck's workshop and see the coffin Buck had made for him.

The door was open, but Buck was not there. In a corner there was a white pine wood box, standing like a cupboard. I went and told Ebenezer I had seen it. He asked me what I thought of it. I said it looked fine. He said, "When the Indians come in thousands, which they will one day, Buck won't have enough wood to go around."

That night I dreamed I was with Hurley. We were being chased by soldiers. One carried a branding iron, with the letter *D.* Then, the soldiers were being chased by Indians, and, instead of running away, Hurley and I were digging holes, and Buck Riley was hammering pine wood boxes—many holes, many boxes. I woke sweating, and thought I could smell Ebenezer's baccy.

A L I C E

As I came from the store one day, a woman called Lorrie Shaw was standing at her gate. She was a big, burly woman, and Bessie used to say she guessed she had hair on her chest. I thought she was waiting to say something to me, and she was. "That squaw livin' with you, she should go back where she came from."

"We like her livin' with us," I said.

"She's brung enough trouble."

"She's the one who's had the trouble."

"Bullshit," she said.

"That ain't a nice thing to say." I had carried on walking. Now I was turning to her.

"It ain't meant to be a nice thing t' say," she said.

I turned away. I said, "Bullshit" to her, in my head.

Cappy

I dug Ebenezer's grave in the place he chose. He said it was the best he'd ever had or was ever likely to get. He asked me what my charge was. I said Dolly Emms had paid me two dollars for her latrine. He said he couldn't pay latrine prices. I said he should pay me whatever he thought right.

"Four dollars, not a cent more or less." He laughed. "It's a topsy-turvy world."

He laughed, and spluttered over his pipe, then went serious. "Cappy-boy, take that young squaw back to her people. This ain't the place for her."

He looked down into the grave again.

"You'll live years yet," I said.

"Put me a foot deeper, an' I'll give you another dollar."

I said I would. We walked back together. It was slow going. He stopped a time or two to light his pipe, and once to stand looking across the hill in silence. Then he said what he had said before.

"When the Indians come in thousands, which they will one day, Buck won't have enough wood to go around."

We walked on.

"Old men repeat theirselves," he said.

Chapter 20

What Happened to Charlie Cruz?

Miss Todd was lying in her hammock, in the shade of an apple tree. One arm was trailing down over the side. In the other was a book. But the book had fallen forward on her face. It covered her mouth and half of her nose. Her eyes were closed. In case she was not asleep, I put my fingers on my lips, to tell Two Songs to be silent. When we were well past the white fence, I told her the joke on the teacher's name, Todd and Toad, and she understood. I thought that was quite amazing, but Two Songs was always amazing.

The sun was high, the August heat was tremendous. There was a shimmer of heat or light coming up from everything. We came to the rocks around the Forbidden Place and sat in the cool of a shadow for a few minutes before following the path to the pool. We could hear the shrill voices of some girls already there. Somewhere above, there was the voice of one of the sentries, loud and deep, and going on and on like he was telling some tale. I couldn't tell the words, but I lay back with amusement at the thought that he was giving an account of some clever thing he had done. It seemed so funny— impress, impress, the way boys do. And it felt good to be stretching out there listening to something that was amusing to listen to, even if it couldn't be heard properly, with my friend beside me.

I closed my eyes, just to enjoy being happy. I heard Two Songs pluck a stalk of grass from near my head, and after a pause I felt it tickle my face, then touch into my nose. I gave a screech and grabbed her arm, and we wrestled a bit. She said, "Swim?" I nodded. We scrambled up, and went along the narrow path between rocks.

One of the sentries must have heard my screech. I saw a shadow move on the rocks to our left, and looked up. There on the top of the steep rock to the right was the head of Charlie Cruz. He was at the level he was supposed to be, partway up the outside of the slope. But it was startling to look up and see him peering down. It was only a moment. He ducked away, and his shadow was gone.

It was not spying, just curiosity about the screech. You couldn't imagine Charlie Cruz bothering to spy. Any boy with about fifty sisters wasn't likely to be special curious over girls. But it was just as well he ducked back, anyway. When I looked to the path again Two Songs was pulling her dress over her head. Then, with a run, she was around the last turn of the path, and I heard the sound of her dive.

The other girls stood to watch, two on the bank, two in the water. Two Songs appeared on the far side of the pool. She waved a greeting, then slipped under the surface again. She went deep, and we lost sight of her. I thought everyone was a bit scared by her daring, as I was, and there were shouts of pleasure when she broke the surface, gasping.

It was a good afternoon of friendship. We could not have guessed the way it would end.

After about an hour we were tired. A small chip of rock came off the cliff above us. Nobody was swimming, and everything was quiet. Even our voices were stilled, after all the cries and shouts. The chip tumbled from ledge to ledge, and stopped just short of the pool. By then we were all looking up to where it came from.

The first thing we saw was the head of Charlie Cruz. Then he stood up and started climbing down the ledges. At the same time, two other boys stood in the pathway.

The girls were shouting, part angry, maybe part amused, scrambling for their clothes. I looked across the pool to Two Songs. She was sitting in a shadow, absolutely still.

Just as I remembered her dress was at the edge of the pathway, one of the boys seized it. He laughed and held it up, and danced behind it. The other boy grabbed it from him and did the same. They passed it between them, taking turns to dance with it, barging among the girls.

Charlie Cruz had reached the ground. Without looking at the girls nearby, he scrambled over the poolside rocks toward Two Songs. She stood, and ran from him. Then she saw there was no way of escape, so she dove into the water.

The girls shouted to Charlie to leave her be, but his friends urged him on. Charlie untied his boots and kicked them off. With a shout, as Two Songs swam in the middle of the pool, he dove. He struck out toward her, but Two Songs glided away, out of sight.

When she came up, she was a good way off from him, but he again struck out, and Two Songs again went down.

This time Charlie judged which way she had gone. When we saw her rising, we shouted to her that he was near, and the boys shouted to him to get her. As she looked across the surface, she screamed something at him, and something at us, and put her arms straight up, to drop down deep. Charlie struggled to pull off his shirt, which was hampering him. When it came off, he flung it away, and it spread on the water for a bit. He shouted something to us that I couldn't make out, but it made the boys laugh. He saw where Two Songs was coming up, and struck out toward her.

The girls were kind of laughing and shouting for him to stop at the same time. We didn't know what we were watching. We didn't know whether it was stupid fun or something more than should be happening there. It was Charlie Cruz, not some stranger.

It was Charlie Cruz, and now he grabbed at Two Songs's hair as she tried to dive away. He caught it and held on. He went with her a bit, holding on. She screamed, and he reached out and held her body. She was still swimming away, with her arms striking forward. Charlie held her waist and went with her, his legs kicking out behind. It was still part-funny, two people making one swimmer.

Then Two Songs went limp. Her arms were still, her head sideways. She was gasping for breath. It looked like Charlie was taken by surprise. He tried to turn her to face him. But suddenly Two Songs put her head and arms down, and kicked wildly. She was taking Charlie down with her. He could go down or let go, and he went down.

On the bank, we were silent. There was nothing to see but the sunlight flashing on the ripples.

"She's drowned him," one of the boys said.

Then Charlie's arms and head came up. He gasped, and sank again, then Two Songs came up beside him. She looked at him, and called to us. It was something we could not make out, but we knew Charlie needed help. One of the boys took his boots off and dove in. The other boy was still holding Two Songs's dress. I took it from him.

"She's nearly drowned him," he said.

I went around the pool to where Two Songs was pulling Charlie against the bank. She scrambled up. I held out the dress, and she put it on. We pulled Charlie out of the water, with the boy helping from underneath.

Charlie's face was terrible pale. He was moaning, and his eyes were closed. His pants were down, tangled about his ankles. Two Songs said something. She turned him over and knelt beside him, pushing down on his back to make water come out of his mouth.

Everyone was standing around. The boy went back in the pool and found Charlie's shirt. The other one talked to Charlie and told him he would be okay. Somebody said keep him warm, so we gave bits of our clothes to cover him. Somebody took his pants and beat the water from them against a rock, and put them in the sun to dry. We had covered him now, but were all thinking of how we had seen him naked.

"It was his own fault," somebody said.

We said it was. We said we should not talk about it to anybody.

"It was just fooling," said one of the boys.

We said it was. But we knew we were not sure. We knew that something in Charlie or something in Two Songs had made it happen. One of the girls asked if anyone knew what Charlie had been going to do. We said nobody knew that. Somebody asked what Two Songs had done to him.

She was sitting alone. She had her head on her knees, and was hugging her ankles. I knew she was crying to herself, the way she did when she sat by Burkhart's grave. I went and put my arm across her shoulders.

The boys said they would stay with Charlie for a while. He was warming in the sun. He would be okay. They handed us our bits of clothes, and we left.

"He just tried to kiss her," one called.

"We know that," I called back.

"It ain't true," one of the girls said to me.

"I suppose it ain't," I said.

We let the girls get ahead of us. When we reached the settlement, they were gone from sight.

Miss Todd was still in her hammock, but now she was reading. She didn't notice us going by.

Chapter 21

THE HEART'S REASONS

"Charlie Cruz was naked," Alice said.

She was in disgrace for taking Two Songs to the Forbidden Place. Without that, Two Songs would never have tried to drown Charlie.

The story had gone around the settlement in a few hours. One of the girls had let it out. Charlie said nothing until his father belted him and made him say the squaw had tried to drown him. He said he was only fooling with her, but the girl's account said more than that. When Bessie and Mama questioned Alice, she didn't say much, but she told me the whole story, or as far as she could tell. She said there were things she was not sure of. She said there were things only Charlie or Two Songs might be sure of. And when Two Songs was questioned, she decided to forget all the English language she knew.

Alice seemed more bothered with Charlie being

naked than anything else. She was embarrassed to tell, and I was kind of embarrassed to listen. She didn't know what had happened under the water.

But there was something that bothered me much more. People were saying the squaw should go back where she came from. Old Ebenezer had said it to me out of kindness. He was sorry for a girl away from her people. Now the voices were against her for other reasons. Indians only bring trouble, they said. The squaw was the cause of Burkhart's death. She was the cause of the flaming arrows and the burning cabin. Now she had nearly drowned Charlie Cruz.

When I went into Dolly Emms's store, I caught part of a conversation that was going on. It seemed like something was being said against Burkhart. I heard someone say his name as I opened the door.

"The dog don't mate with the jackal," someone said.

Dolly Emms said something about "young ears," and they went confused, and started talking about everything under the sun except Burkhart and Two Songs. Only Lorrie Shaw stuck with what she wanted to say.

"I'm amazed she's given houseroom," she said.

Dolly Emms said something that sounded good, the way she often did. "The heart has its reasons."

I liked that, and said it over as I dug the extra foot in

Ebenezer's grave. As I worked, I knew that the time would come soon when I would take Two Songs to her people. I didn't know where they were, but I could find out. Two Songs had already made the journey in the opposite direction. And I knew that I would also try to find Hurley, if the soldiers hadn't found him already.

I was remembering something. The night I listened at my open wall cupboard to Lieutenant Malone talking to Bessie about places they had both known, he told about a boy called Auguste Chouteau. He was only thirteen, but he was the chief helper of the man who founded the city of St. Louis.

When the digging was done, I climbed out of the hole and went over to Burkhart. He was under a mound that was trying to be green in spite of the August sun. I told him I would take Two Songs to her people when she needed to go.

Then I went to Ebenezer to tell him his grave was dug. He was sitting on a bench, watching Buck at work. He said, with a grin at Buck, that he had forgotten how much he had agreed to pay.

I said, "Four dollars, and one more for the extra foot."

"Not a cent more, not a cent less," he said. He went into the house and fetched five dollars.

I asked Buck if he could teach me to cut letters into wood. He said yes, if I would come sometime when he wasn't busy. He asked me what I wanted to cut. I said Burkhart's grave marker.

"You don't have to wait for Buck," said Ebenezer.

He pulled about among already smoothed pieces of wood. He chose two, and called me over to a bench.

"This one for practice. This one for the job."

Buck passed him a pencil and a steel ruler. He took the pencil, passed the ruler back. He pulled my sleeve. "Just watch."

He started to draw the letters. I was amazed at the sharp, clear lines from the old hand. He repeated two of them on the spare piece. He said I could do the rest if I needed them. "But you won't," he said. "Just watch."

He took a mallet and chisel, and started to cut the spare wood. He told me to watch the angle of the chisel. After a few minutes, he put the tools into my hands and told me to carry on. After a while, he said I could start on the best board in the morning.

In the morning, I cut BURKHART.

Buck said, "When you want to do something well, you can do it well."

He asked me what dates I wanted to put. I didn't

know the year Burkhart was born. He said I could just put the year he died. Ebenezer said there should be a word or two underneath. One would do. I told him the word and he marked it out in pencil.

I cut ARTIST.

Chapter 22

TOUCHING GOODBYE

Long Shadow knew where Two Songs was living. One night an arrow struck above the shutters of my window. The light of flames was bright through the slats.

I took the stairs two at a time and fetched a mop handle. I opened one shutter slightly, swung a whack at the arrow, and sent it falling. Just then, there was a whinny from the stable. Long Shadow was after the horses. I pulled the derringer from my pants on the bedside chair, opened the shutter, and fired into the darkness. The sound of the shot must have been enough to make Long Shadow change his mind. I could see that he leaped the fence and ran toward the copse.

The sound of the shot had wakened the house. We found there was another flaming arrow over the window of a guest room. I went in and knocked it away. A terrified old man sat up in bed to watch, while his wife put her head under the bedclothes. He said he had never seen a flaming arrow before. He asked if we got many. I said not many. Bessie made me apologize in the morning for not telling him it was the first time the Eldo house had had any.

He was an Englishman. He said, "I was bloody scared." He had come to the West to find his long-lost brother. He said he thought his brother was a traveling salesman. "Really bloody scared," he said again. He wasn't sure his brother was worth the bother.

While we were at breakfast, some women came knocking at the door to say that the squaw should leave Buffalo Sky. Long Shadow and his friends had stolen or tried to burn in a dozen places. Mama shut the kitchen door and went to talk out in the yard. When she came in she wouldn't say much.

Two Songs had changed since what had happened at the Forbidden Place. I thought she was blaming Alice for taking her there. Now, she wanted to go off alone, riding her pony. I was afraid she might be thinking she should give herself to Long Shadow. I said I would ride with her if she would like that. Maybe she was glad to be stopped from doing what she was thinking. She said yes.

We rode over the hill to the derelict cabin. Then we went on down the slope. At the bottom, she dismounted. She left her pony grazing and came to me.

"I ride him?" she asked.

I slid down. She mounted, and circled around a while, walking. She smiled at me and went forward to the place under the trees where she had sat on that day when I watched Burkhart drawing her. She stopped the stallion, and sat there. The light touched into the shadows around her, just as it had then. I stood and watched, waiting until she wanted to turn. I tried to think what might be in her thoughts, but my own feelings came rushing in.

"Draw." I whispered Burkhart's order. "I can't," I said.

Two Songs turned the stallion and rode toward me. She was smiling, but tears were running.

"A good place, Cappy," she said. She jumped down. "You like this place. You like this good place always."

I said yes.

She said, "Come." She took my hand, and we went to where she had sat on the horse. She went to the nearest tree, and spread her arms as far as they would go around it, and put an ear to its smooth bark. She turned, and indicated that I should touch the tree and listen to it too. I felt foolish, but I wanted to please her. The rush of blood in my ears sounded like the rush of sap in the tree. But there was more than the rush of blood, and I thought I was listening to the sound of the tree.

GOODBYE, BUFFALO SKY

In words that came slowly, she told me that when her people had to leave a place they loved, they liked to touch it. It made the place come with them on their journey. She touched some leaves overhead, the stallion's hoof marks in the earth, a broken twig. It seemed a silly kind of thing, but I followed her, and she was pleased. Then I realized that by these actions she was telling me that she was leaving.

"Don't go away," I said.

Her eyes were full of tears again.

"I have to go away."

We walked the horses up to the derelict cabin. Two Songs was smiling now.

"Come out of there." She tried Burkhart's voice. We laughed. The she leaped onto the pony's back, and cantered up the slope.

She stopped at the top, waiting for me to follow. I looked up at her, against the clear blue sky, and thought it was the last time I would see her like that.

I started to follow, but she kicked her heels into the pony's flanks, and was gone from sight. When I reached the top she was well away, riding across the hill. I followed, and she turned up higher, riding across the top of the hill. It was a game, riding along and down and around again. We played it for the good feeling of being together, but also the feeling of doing something for the last time.

She dismounted by the copse. We stood silent a while. The horses steamed and shook off flies.

As we went to the stable, I said I would come with her to find her people. She said, "Bessie?" I said Bessie would understand.

Chapter 23

THE RAWHIDE WHIP

Cappy told me he was going with Two Songs. I said she didn't need to go. He said she did, and I was not to tell anyone he was going too. He made me promise. I started to put together a few things they would need for the journey.

They would go on the horses. They would drag the tepee behind the pony, Indian-fashion, with the poles spread apart to hold their supplies. Cappy called it a "travois." He asked if I knew that word. I said yes, because there was no need to show I was ignorant. But I felt guilty at having to deceive Mama and Bessie about the preparations.

Then something happened that made the journey begin before Cappy intended.

Two Songs was in the yard, at the water pump, with pails for the horses. I was in the outhouse when she screamed. I ran out and saw Lorrie Shaw and Charlie Cruz's mother dragging Two Songs out of the gate. Out-

94

side the gate, there were women with sticks, some of Charlie's grown-up sisters. As soon as they had Two Songs outside, they started to lay into her. She kicked and screamed, and pulled away, and ran toward the copse. I screamed at them, but they followed her, shouting, "Get the squaw."

There was an old rawhide whip on the beams of the stable. I ran and got it, and followed to the copse. In a clearing, they had Two Songs on the ground. They were standing over her, screeching and jeering, and Lorrie Shaw was jumping in and hitting her, then standing back and letting the sisters have a turn.

I shouted at them, swung the whip, and hit three at one go. They were so surprised, they fell aside. I lashed at each of them again. I was mad scared, and that angry I didn't care what I did. I lashed and lashed till they dropped right back, and Two Songs scrambled away and ran out onto the hill on the far side of the copse.

Lorrie Shaw stood facing me, with the others behind her. I held the rawhide out to the side, ready to use it if she made a move.

"We done what we wanted," she said. "And we'll git you another day, Missie."

I was mad scared, but I didn't give her any worth just then.

"Try now," I said. "Just try now. See what you get."

"I can wait," she said. "I can wait a while, girlie."

The others were pulling back. She knew I wouldn't come at her from behind now, so she turned away. They started to talk loudly, circling off around me through the trees, talking dirty about Two Songs and Burkhart, and Mama and Bessie, and me. I said not a word back, but looked at the rawhide whip lying like a thin snake, and thought it was a fine friend. Then I ran to find Two Songs.

She had come down to the edge of the copse. She was holding cool leaves on her sore places. We hugged a bit, then stretched out on our backs, looking at the sky. There were two small clouds chasing across the blue. I thought they might be horses. There was a single rider on one, two on the other. I watched them go, on and on to the blurry distance.

Chapter 24

AWAY

We started soon after breakfast. Mama Eldo and Bessie saw us off. Alice said her tearful goodbyes to Two Songs indoors. Two Songs had gone through the house touching goodbye to things in the Indian way, and finished by touching the outhouse door. She told Mama she would come back one day to collect some of her possessions. A few small things were packed on the travois. I had wrapped three of Burkhart's sketchbooks in oilskin to keep them from damage, but all the paintings, except a few watercolors, had to be left. I had promised to turn back after two or three days, when Two Songs was into Indian country. I felt a bit sick at heart because I knew it was a promise I was going to break.

We made good progress, but we were mostly silent. We were so full of feelings, we just didn't know what to say. A few people had stood nearly silent in the road as we left the settlement. I thought they might be feeling not too sure about the way Two Songs was driven out. Dolly

Emms made us wait while she piled some provisions into a pack. She said, "I told you that you would be more than just a latrine digger." Then she said, "Come back someday." I wondered how she was able to guess what was in my mind about not turning back.

Traveling was slow with the travois dragging behind the pony, but we had reached the second northward turn soon after noon. It was open country, but we found a group of trees for shade. We ate some bread and drank from the creek.

Beyond the creek was a hill. It was the same hill I had seen the Indians racing across on the day I dug the latrine. We were now on its far side, and had spent the morning following the creek around it. There was a ferry on the settlement side, another near the place we were now resting. In the dazzle of sunlight, I could see the small path that came across the dip at the center of the hill, leading down to the ferry.

There was a tiny figure on the path. Its smallness gave some idea of the size of the hill. Though it was coming downward, it hardly seemed to get bigger as I watched. This was a figure on foot, but I wondered what our own progress would be in the landscapes we had to travel. I had no clear idea of what might lie ahead. Though there would be no mountains, each new distance, as it came into view beyond a hill or ridge, might be vast. And I had little notion of what creatures or humans might be in our way.

Two Songs had some idea of where the tribe had been camped when she left with Burkhart in the spring. But now they would be elsewhere, following their food, the buffalo. And it was no longer possible for them to know for sure where the herds might be. The white man had killed off so many buffalo with his guns, everyone was now saying that soon there would be few left. Travelers said the prairies were strewn with great white skeletons.

We had spent so much time fixing the tepee as a travois, and loading it, and making other preparations, that we had gone to bed late. Now, tiredness caught up with us, and we stretched out to rest a while in shade before going on in the afternoon sun. I was soon dozing, lying on my back, with Two Songs face downward nearby, the sound of the horses grazing half drawing me back to wakefulness once or twice. I dreamed we were searching for Burkhart, but he kept chuckling and saying we would never find him.

"Where are you?" I asked. My voice seemed louder than I intended, and it startled me awake.

I opened my eyes, remembered where I was. Two Songs and Alice were standing over me, holding close, side by side, smiling and tearful together.

Chapter 25

SINGING STRANGER

I told Alice she was mad to come.

She said, "I've always been a bit mad."

"I know that," I said. "Where's your horse?"

"Over there." She pointed to the stallion. "I'll sit up behind you."

"You can walk," I said. "Did you tell Mama you were coming?"

"I left a note."

I wanted to tell her the problem was that I was not going back after three days. But I had planned to make it seem I decided that when the time came. I wanted it to seem like the right thing to do. I hoped it would be the right thing.

"Supposin' we don't turn back after three days?" I said.

It took her by surprise.

"Why not?"

"Might be reasons. Might be best you go back now."

"I want to come along," she said. She pouted. "I reckon you planned to go more than three days."

We moved on through the afternoon, keeping by the bank of the stream. Alice sat up behind me. It was a well-worn track, wide enough for Two Songs to ride alongside. Out in that great country our voices seemed so small and lost. We didn't talk much, except in snatches.

After an hour or two, Alice tried to get us singing. She started on "Oh! Susanna," singing happily to herself for a couple of verses, then telling me to join in. I tried a bit, and it sounded good, with our voices going together. I don't know what the stallion made of it, but he seemed to be listening, with his ears pricked up. Two Songs was amused, and Alice told her to sing. She did a line at a time, trying to get Two Songs to join in on a repeat. In a short while we were all singing the first verse.

"I came from Alabama wid a banjo on my knee,
I'm gwan to Louisiana
My true love for to see,
It rained all night the day I left,
The weather it was dry,
The sun so hot I froze to death;
Susanna don't you cry."

We had come to a stretch where the track was raised somewhat higher above the waters, and further from the edge. We could only see the stream through gaps in clusters of bushes. We were having great fun with the song, going over and over the part Two Songs was able to sing. She was very happy with it, even if some of the words didn't mean much to her. Then, when we came to the end of a verse, and paused to rest our voices, we were amazed to hear the song going on from somewhere below, on the other side of the bushes.

We pulled up. It was no echo, because the words were different. The stallion's ears were up.

They twitched, and he snorted. Alice squeezed my waist, and giggled. Two Songs was staring into the bushes. The singing stopped at the end of the verse.

I slipped down from the stallion and went to the bushes. Just beyond them, I was looking down on the canvas cover of a small cart. It was like a very small wagon. Two horses were grazing, one in the shafts, one tied behind. A ruddy-faced man was sitting on the ground nearby, beside a small blaze, drinking from a tin mug.

"Hallo, there," he called. "Nice singing! Drive on for fifty yards and you'll find a way down here. It's a good stopping place. Come and join me."

We found the way down. He stood as we approached.

He was a healthy-looking man, used to the open air. His suit was old, and had been smart, a Sunday suit. The jacket was trailing on the ground from one finger through a loop. He put it on and came over, and offered his hand to me as I dismounted.

"Welcome. My name is Partington."

I told him my name. As I introduced Alice and Two Songs, he took the hand of each and kissed the back of it. They were surprised and amused. He said we must have some coffee with him. I remembered the frightened old man with his wife in the Eldo guest room. His name was Partington too.

Painted on the cart cover in black was "Saucepan Partington." Around the wooden sides there were pots and pans of various sizes, hanging by their handles from hooks. Others hung inside the cover.

There was coffee in his pot. He poured it into tin mugs like his own. We didn't care much for it, but tried not to let him see.

I said, "I think I've seen your brother."

"My . . . brother . . ." He said it slowly. It seemed that he couldn't believe what I had said.

"Maybe, he could've been," I said.

I told him about the old man and his wife. He wanted to know everything I could tell him. Did I know his first name? What name did he call his wife? How was he traveling? How long was he staying? Where was he going next? Would he be a man of seventy years? His wife about five years younger? Was he bald? Was his voice high pitched for a man? Womanish? Did he say how long he had been in this country? Did I think that the old man actually *looked* enough like himself to be his brother? Was he a carefully dressed man, in spite of all his journeying? Did he look as if he might live a good many years yet? Did he mention the actual place he came from in England?

My answers were not able to prove to him that the old man was his brother. I didn't know his first name, or his wife's, or where he came from. But my answers to the other questions made him feel sure my guess was right.

"It would be Richard," he said. "Yes, it would be Dickie."

He asked again how long I thought Dickie would be staying. I said it would be another day or two. Visitors liked the Eldo house, and sometimes stayed longer than they intended. And it wasn't always possible to get seats on the stagecoach.

"Who would have thought it—Dickie coming three thousand miles of ocean and two thousand more on land, just to find *me*?"

I said it was some journey for an old man. His eyes suddenly filled with tears. He tried to say something, but was overcome by feelings. He stood, and climbed into his cart, and didn't come out for a while. We felt uneasy, and talked about things that didn't matter at all. When he appeared, he brought some oatmeal cakes in a tin.

"I'm failing in courtesy," he said. "I do apologize."

Alice said we understood. I thought she sounded just like Bessie. She didn't only know the right thing to say, she meant it too.

He boiled the kettle again while we ate oatmeal cakes. He said he had noticed we were "not very partial" to his coffee, so this time he would make tea. As we sat around to drink it, he told us about the places he traveled, and we told him of our journey. He had joined the trail we were on only a few miles ahead. Something had made him turn right, southward, instead of left.

"Our meeting is fortuitous," he said. "If I had turned north, we might never have met. We could have gone on apart for ever and ever, Amen. Think of that. Four souls who love singing 'Susanna,' and never destined to meet! But Fate had a guiding hand today, my young friends."

He seemed a very odd man, but very likable. It was good to be with him. When he said that this was a good place for making camp, and that it would be sensible to put up our tepee early, because of the way sunset came down so quickly, we agreed to camp with him. He said he would make a start soon after dawn and travel on to the settlement. What a surprise was in store for his brother!

Two Songs put up the tepee. She showed Alice how it should be done. I watered the horses. Our new friend brought out two rabbits he had snared early that morning. He prepared them for the cooking pot, and Two Songs served us a meal inside the tepee. I felt sad and didn't want much to eat, because it was the first time I had been in the tepee since I found Burkhart with the arrow through him. The hole in the hide was still there. If I moved my head to the right place, I could make a star stand in the dead center. I wondered if Burkhart was up there somewhere, watching. I tried to think of his face, but it was no longer sharp and clear to me.

Our friend said his brother was an English "Sir." After Dickie's death, he would be expected to take the title himself, but he didn't want to be "Sir." And he had always been embarrassed by his own Christian names, so he wouldn't tell us what they were. He liked to be called what he was called now, Saucepan Partington. If we liked, we could call him S. P.

He went out and stoked the fire to a good blaze. We sat round it. He said we should sing "Oh! Susanna" together. He started it, and we joined in. We sang it over and over, having great fun. The fire was hot on our faces, but our backs soon got cold. We all faced outward for a while, and sang "Susanna" into the dark. Creatures called back to us.

We went into the tepee, and Saucepan brought more tea. After that, he poured himself a glass of whiskey and said we were sensible to refuse it. Then he sang us some songs he remembered from long ago.

When we were ready to sleep, he said he would sleep in his cart to keep his saucepans company.

"I must think what I shall say to Dickie tomorrow," he said. He seemed worried. He stood in the entrance of the tepee, with his whiskey bottle in his hand, down by his leg. "I want you to know that you are the most engaging young people I have ever met." He turned away. "Oh, perhaps I should let old Dickie travel on looking for me. Would it be better that way?" He stood a moment longer, as if trying to answer his own question. "Good night, good friends," he said.

I lay thinking how the old man in the Eldo house had said he wondered if his long-lost brother was really worth searching for. I thought he was.

Chapter 26

SPYGLASS AND TRUTH MAN

We slept a bit cold. I woke several times before dawn, and Alice was awake too. Two Songs was used to sleeping on the ground, so she was more comfortable. When the rising sun was on the tepee, we warmed up and went into a deep sleep.

"Are you awake?"

It was Saucepan, from outside. I woke, and saw Two Songs sitting up, combing her hair. Alice roused.

"Just awake," I called.

"Cappy, come over to the cart when you're ready," Saucepan said.

When I went to him, he said he had been walking around and had seen there were some soldiers camped on the higher ground a little way ahead. A few had come down to bathe in the creek. They had now gone back up.

"The spyglass can become a habit out here in the wilderness," he said. He took a spyglass from his jacket.

"Could you ask the young ladies to cook porridge? The fire's lit. There's a bag of oats in the cart. And they should be able to find a saucepan."

I took the message to Alice, and told her about the soldiers. She was excited at the idea that they might be Lieutenant Malone's boys.

I went with Saucepan. When the soldiers' camp was in sight we hid in bushes. After looking through the spyglass he handed it to me.

The camp seemed to jump forward. The tents seemed only a few yards off. I could see steam coming up from a horse's pee. There were only five small tents, of the bivouac kind, arranged around a campfire. A supplies wagon was close by. I recognized the men.

I put the spyglass slowly over the whole scene a second time, looking for Long Shadow or Hurley. I thought any prisoner might be chained to a cartwheel. Nobody was.

Over breakfast, we told Saucepan about the soldiers, Hurley, Long Shadow, and Burkhart. He asked questions about all of them. He was especially interested in Burkhart.

"I've made a few drawings myself as I've traveled around," he said, "but I'm not a real artist like your friend." He smiled, a bit sadly. "I sometimes wonder if

I'm a real anything."

He hadn't mentioned his brother. I asked how soon he would set off to meet him. He frowned. "It could be some time. I thought about it in the small hours of the night. It isn't the simple matter it might seem to be. I can't explain. Yes, it could be some time."

"But he might be gone."

He looked at us, to see what we thought. "I know. I hope you don't think badly of me."

We said no. Two Songs surprised us by saying something more. "You, Mister Saucepan, are a very nice truth man. Burkhart was a very nice truth man." We were silent while she tried to find another word she wanted. Then it came, and her eyes were bright with tears. "Also."

Saucepan said, "You are very kind. Very kind and very beautiful."

Two Songs was suddenly very happy to speak her new language. She looked at Alice. "Alice like speak with soldiers."

Saucepan smiled, and said, "Ah!"

★
★ ★

Chapter 27

PRETTY RIBBONS

Cappy went up to the army camp with Saucepan in his cart. Saucepan said he would try to sell his wares to the soldiers. Besides his pots and pans, he carried all sorts of useful things, from brushes, combs, and razors, to ladies' bonnets and unmentionables.

After they went, I helped Two Songs take down the tepee and fix it ready for travel. Then we fed and watered the horses, and after that we sat by a rock on the edge of the creek. I had asked Cappy to tell Corporal Dancy where I would be.

I watched him coming from way off. He was dressed in pants and shirt, without his jacket or cap. He was swinging along, pulling stalks of grass here and there, looking down and around, everywhere except to where we were sitting. I was kind of nervous too, wondering what we could talk about.

I thought, he is older than I am, so he should really

know what to say, shouldn't he? But really I knew he wouldn't. He might have been in battles, and even killed people, and traveled this wide land in places I never heard of. But that didn't make it any easier for him to talk with a girl if he was shy and still a boy in his heart. That was a strange thing, wasn't it? Maybe it was good too, because it made us the same in our feelings. I didn't mind being shy with him at all really, so long as I would know something of what to say, and didn't get tongue-tied because I'd said something that sounded young and silly or pretending to be older and smarter than I was.

Then he was near, at the bottom of the slope, and looking at us. He waved, and I waved back, and he came on quickly. He had little presents in his hand, two little presents in tissue paper. Instead of greeting us properly first, he couldn't wait to give them over, one for each of us, as soon as he was in reach. I loved that. I knew I didn't have to think about wanting him to be sweet on me.

"They ain't much," he said. "I just bought 'em from that Saucepan fella. Hope you like 'em."

They were pretty hair ribbons, tied in bows, light blue, on little fasteners. Fine for both of us, the black of Two Songs's tresses, the middish brown of mine. We fixed them for each other right away, thanking Dan and showing our pleasure. He stood grinning, with a red face, pleased with his choice for sure.

"You ain't swimmin'," he said. "I didn't know if you'd be swimmin'."

I knew straightway that he was remembering the talk we'd cut ourselves short in some weeks back, about how he should see Two Songs bathing, and how we were both too shy for that conversation. Now, as soon as he had said, "You ain't swimmin'," he knew he had said it too early, too straight out. Instead of having a nice joke, he had embarrassed himself, and I felt sorry for him.

"Not today," I said. But that sounded too sharp. "Some other time, maybe," I said. It sounded better.

He was happy with that escape.

"You both look real nice in them ribbons," he said. "I guessed you might wear ribbons sometime."

Two Songs touched my back. She didn't need to say anything. She moved off a bit, to leave me free to talk alone with Dan.

We sat on a ledge of rock, facing over the creek. The sun made a dazzle on the water.

"We bin movin' around a lot," he said. "Most every day we bin ridin'. I kinda missed you."

"I missed you."

"That's how it is, I guess."

"I know," I said.

"Would be good to stay in one place a bit," he said. "It was good, stayin' your house."

113

"Soldier's job, movin' on," I said. I was remembering what Bessie said.

"I was thinkin' about your mama's place a lot."

"What did you think about it?"

"Mostly you, I guess."

He took a glance at me. I was looking into the dazzle of the water, but I knew he looked at me. I leaned a bit to him, and he put his arm across the back of my waist.

"I was hopin' you'd come back," I said. "I'm that pleased to see you again."

"Which way you bin ridin'?" he asked.

"North."

"We're turnin' north," he said.

Two Songs had turned and was smiling at us. Dan took his arm from my back.

"Two Songs looks nice in your ribbons," I said.

"You look real pretty in yours," he said. He stood up. "I must go."

The waters dazzled patterns on his face. He stood, not knowing what more to say. I didn't know what more to say either. I thought I could ask about the soldiers chasing Long Shadow and Hurley, but it would be too many words. We just stood a moment. He picked up a sliver of rock and made it skim across the water. I thought how it was called making ducks and drakes, but I didn't say a word.

"Lieutenant's keen on chasin' that Long Shadow," Dan said. He looked at me, serious. "I'll tell you somethin' else. He's keen on catchin' that Hurley fella too."

When Dan had gone, I went with Two Songs back to the horses. She held up a little piece of mirror she had, so we could look at our ribbons. But I wasn't thinking anymore about pretty ribbons. I was thinking of soldiers chasing Hurley.

Chapter 28

THE SKULL

We started to ride north with the soldiers. Lieutenant Malone said we should ride out in front so we were not in the clouds of dust that came up from the hooves. Once in a while, he sent a scout ahead to look for signs of danger.

He had sent another soldier galloping back to the settlement. He was to tell Mama Eldo that Alice and I were not returning as soon as expected, because we could travel under army protection. We were safe with him, and he would bring us back as soon as possible.

Lieutenant Malone was displeased with us. He said that to send a messenger was the best he could do if we insisted on riding for several days before leaving Two Songs. He had told us to go back straightway. He would look after Two Songs. I said I had made a promise to Burkhart.

"Burkhart's dead," he said.

I said I had made a promise over his grave.

"Graveyard promises fall on deaf ears," he said.

In my head, I said his words fell on deaf ears too. I felt a bit sick at heart, because I knew he was only concerned for our safety. But he had asked Saucepan if he had ever come across an army deserter called Hurley. Saucepan had said no. I decided then that I wanted to take whatever chance might come to warn Hurley of the danger he was in. And I was beginning to be sick at the idea of leaving Two Songs. I wondered if I would ever see her again.

Saucepan was silent much of the time. He seemed deep in his thoughts, and I guessed his thoughts were far away. I wondered if he was feeling bad about not going to meet his brother. Perhaps they had never been very friendly in their lives of long ago. Perhaps there had been some quarrel. It seemed a sad thing for old Dickie to come so far to find him, and to be so near to doing it, and then for Saucepan to avoid him—and to feel bad about it too. Now, perhaps, they would never meet again.

We made our own small campfire apart from the soldiers. When Alice and Two Songs had gone into the tepee, ready for sleep after a long day riding in the sun, I sat in the dark with Saucepan. He poked a stick to stir the dying embers.

"It's too late," he said.

"You want to turn in?" I asked.

"No, I don't mean that kind of late, Cappy. I was thinking of old Dickie." He paused, and I thought he was trying to find a way of explaining, but he only said, "Years . . . years too late."

I wanted to start him thinking about something else. I said I was bothered that Lieutenant Malone now seemed keen to catch my friend Hurley. Back at the settlement, one of the soldiers had said he was not that sort of man.

Saucepan said it looked as if the soldiers had been riding for weeks without accomplishing much. Malone needed something to show for all that time in the saddle. Even a poor wretch of a deserter was better than nothing.

"Lieutenants want to be captains," he said. He added that Hurley seemed to be the sort of man he himself would like. "I suppose some people would say I'm a kind of deserter myself. I didn't stay where I was expected to stay. I took off to somewhere more congenial. Yes, I think I would like your Hurley."

In the morning, we came to a place of buffalo skeletons, hundreds of them, spread for as far as we could see. They were whitened by sun and rain, and individual bones had been pulled from the rest when wolves and other creatures had feasted after the hunters had gone.

White hunters usually left almost everything,

Saucepan said. They killed for sport, for the excitement of leveling a gun and bringing down a great wild creature. Often, they were happy to pick off one that was peacefully grazing. But the Indians killed for food, never for the pleasure of the kill. They had the deepest of respect for the buffalo as a fellow creature sharing the earth, and almost every part of the animal became part of their own lives. But nowadays, traders were paying white men and Indians alike to kill for the price of the hides.

I rode beside Saucepan and listened to him talking about the way the Indians thought of the buffalo, and how they used it. His voice drifted out from his cart, to the creaking of wheels, the slap of reins, and the jangling of his saucepans.

"Rawhide for harnesses—

"Tanned hide for tepees, moccasins, robes—

"Fur for blankets, saddle covers, mittens—

"Hair makes strong string, or a soft pillow—

"Shoulder blades make hoes—

"Horns make a headdress, cups, and spoons—

"The skull is painted for dances, rituals—

"The rough tongue makes a hairbrush—

"Bones become knives—

"Hooves make glue, or shape into tools—

"Great ribs become the children's sleds—

"Tendons are bowstrings, threads for sewing—

"The bladder a food bag—

"The tail a fly whisk—

"Old dung makes a campfire—

"One part is not used, left where it lies—

"A heart brings life to the wandering herd."

At sundown, Saucepan lifted a skull onto a standing column of rock, and we watched its long shadow thrown across the prairie. Its eye sockets went dark, as the bone lost its whiteness and took on the red-gold of the sky. Saucepan stood behind it and put his face to the neck hole, and sang a few lines of "Susanna," very soft and ghostly, so his voice came out of the eyes. When he went off, talking with Alice, I stayed a bit longer with Two Songs. I went behind the rock, intending to try my voice inside the skull like Saucepan.

But suddenly the world seemed such a strange place, full of unexpected things, and I was silent. The sky through the eye holes was a deep violet. Two Songs looked in. I could barely see her face, but it was amazing beautiful and sad, and we looked at each other in there for a moment, then she turned away and ran off to catch up with Alice.

★
★ ★

Chapter 29

A DEAD SOLDIER

Dan had been saying for days that Lieutenant Malone was worried because the soldier he sent with a message for Mama had not returned. Private Terry was a good soldier. He would have come straight back. Something must have happened to prevent him from catching up with us. Then, late one afternoon, his horse came cantering into camp, all covered with lather, and terrified. The poor man was slumped across the saddle, tied there. His head and arms hung down on one side, his legs on the other. A swarm of flies had been following the horse. They settled all over as soon as it stopped.

It was the first time I had seen a dead person. It seemed like the worst kind of dead person anyone could see. When they took him off the horse and put him on the ground, someone covered his face with a blanket. But I had seen his face, patched with thick dried blood. I had seen the raw place on top of his head, where his scalp had been sliced off. And his terrible eyes turned upward.

Then one of the soldiers took me by the shoulders and ran me away. He was rough and angry, and told me not to poke my silly little snout where it wasn't wanted. He nearly slung me to the ground in his upset, and left me there.

I just blubbered for a while, but I was kind of glad to be shoved away, really. Then Two Songs came. She pulled me up and took me aside. Cappy was with the soldiers, looking down at the man under the blanket.

Then a couple of soldiers started calling something vile after Two Songs, because of their upset at what Indians had done to their comrade. One broke away from the rest and came behind us, saying things, and lifted up her dress with his riding whip. There was a shout, and Dan Dancy stomped over and ordered the man to stand by Lieutenant Malone's tent. The soldier went off, muttering, and turned back to glare at us. Dan told us he was sorry, but the killing of a comrade in that way was hard for the boys to take.

Now Cappy came. I guessed it was because of the insult to Two Songs. I said about time too, which he didn't like. It was a hard time for all, and Lieutenant Malone was as upset as anyone, because Private Terry had been with him for several years and came from his own hometown. He walked among the tents, slapping at his riding boots with his whip in agitation, then gave an order for a grave to be dug. Dan said the hurry was because wild creatures would be attracted during the night by the scent of blood.

I thought of the happy day when these soldiers had come to our house back home, and some said "Pretty gal" after me. It seemed a long time ago, and Buffalo Sky a great distance away. I felt homesick, and frightened of this land.

The soldiers took turns at digging. When the grave was ready, we gathered around. Lieutenant Malone wanted Two Songs to stand at his side, to show all his men that there should be no feeling against just any Indian because of the deeds of a few. He said that he guessed the man who had killed Private Terry was the man who had killed the husband of this Indian girl. We should all expect him to show himself quite soon, because he would be gloating over his crime. Then, he would be hunted down.

Everybody was grim and silent, except for one young soldier who was snuffling, like I was. The body was lowered into the ground, with the flag wrapped over the blanket. A bugler played while all the soldiers stood at attention and Lieutenant Malone saluted. Then Dan read a prayer, very nervous, with his voice shaky and hurrying. Lieutenant Malone said some good things about

Private Terry, and how much his comrades loved him.

"And I am one of those," he said.

Then something happened that we didn't know about beforehand. Lieutenant Malone said Mister Partington would render a song that was a favorite with Private Terry. And, clear and sweet, sweet, sweet on the evening air, Saucepan sang "Beautiful Dreamer." It seemed like the sweetest song I ever heard, and everyone looked amazed. I saw one poor soldier standing with his mouth wide open. When it was finished, some of the words seemed to float around my head. The moon standing overhead seemed to be the moon in the song.

They started to fill in the grave. We turned away. Lieutenant Malone called over the soldier who had been rude to Two Songs. "Apologize."

The soldier stood in front of Two Songs. "I'm right sorry, ma'am, for what I done," he said. His voice trembled, and suddenly his face cracked up with his feelings.

Two Songs looked at Lieutenant Malone, then she put an arm across the young man's shoulder.

"He's young and foolish," said the lieutenant. Then he apologized to me. He said he didn't mean the young were always foolish.

"Only most of the time," said Saucepan. "Like the rest of us."

Chapter 30

CRONK'S FERRY

We were coming to a settlement called Cronk's Ferry. The idea of being among ordinary people for a few days cheered the soldiers up. They needed supplies, and to take their minds off the death of their comrade. Saucepan was pleased too, at the prospect of sales. We stopped a mile short of Cronk's Ferry for the soldiers to smarten themselves, brushing down uniforms, polishing boots, shaving. I was amused to watch Saucepan bringing out more pots and pans to hang around his cart, ready for the ladies. We rode into the settlement with the clatter and clang of his wares ahead of us.

As soon as we entered the place, we saw that it was a special day of some sort. There were flags out of upstairs windows, stalls for selling or for try-your-luck games, and the main street was fair crowded. From the number of carts and tethered horses, it seemed an attraction for people from miles around, and a small river steamer was alongside the ferry landing at the end of a side street. We had left our creek several days back, and were now on the left bank of the river itself. Saucepan said we would be able to go across on the ferry, which was big enough to carry horses. He knew the settlement from several years before, and some of the ladies who straightway gathered around his cart appeared to remember him.

He was already doing a good trade. With the canvas cover down, he was standing in the middle of the cart, asking ladies to examine the wares, then hold up anything they wanted to buy. When an item was held up, he told the lady to say the marked price. When he heard it, he would say, "I'll take off ten percent for your pretty face," or something similar. "Ten percent off for your golden curls . . . for your brown eyes . . . for your charming bonnet . . . for your silver hair, ma'am . . . for your smile, sweetheart . . ." Everyone had ten percent off.

Some men stood behind the group, laughing, making jokes of their own, amused by Saucepan's enjoyment of his work. I thought they would never guess he was the long-lost brother of old Dickie, an English "Sir," who was searching this land for him.

I could smell the clothes of someone standing near me. I looked at him. He was about sixteen, tall and thin.

Greasy black hair came in straight lengths from under his old brown hat. His front teeth stuck out at the same slope as his long nose.

"Buy yer mama a saucepan, Snapper."

It was from a man behind him. He was short, oldish, with a beaver hat. Snapper turned and grinned. "I might."

I edged away a bit, from the smell. The man looked at me.

"This is Snapper," he said. "Nobody like Snapper fer bitin' the tail off a rat. One snap, and off! You'll see later, won't he, Snapper?"

"Maybe." Snapper grinned. I looked at his teeth.

"He used t' be a little fella when he was young," the man said. "We all used t' say 'Whippersnapper.' Then, sudden-like, he shot up lank and tall, and he jest got called Snapper." He pushed the boy in the back. "Didn't yer, Snapper?"

"So you say," said Snapper.

"Look at them fine teeth," the man said. "Yer need them sort of choppers t' take a tail off neat an' clean."

"Why don't you button up?" said Snapper.

I saw Alice and Two Songs and edged away toward them. They had put on their pretty blue hair ribbons. Dan Dancy joined us, and we went around the stalls, just looking at things. After a while, we tried a game or two. Dan had three swings with a heavy mallet to make a bolt shoot up a pole and ring a bell. The second one did the trick. Alice wanted me to try. I did, and failed. Two Songs said I nearly did it. I knew from her look she had wanted me to beat Dan. I remembered how I told Burkhart that, one day, I would like to be able to draw Two Songs sitting on her pony. That day seemed no more likely now than ringing the bell on the top of this stupid pole.

A white-haired man in a suit stood on a tub and made a speech. He said that everybody knew that this was the thirtieth anniversary of Cronk's Ferry. He was Simon Cronk from St. Louis. Cronk's Ferry had been built by his granddad, William. He said he wondered what his grandfather would have thought of the festivities here today.

An old man standing near me said quietly, "Not much—he was a miserable old swine."

After that there was "The Rat Catch." A short track was made, lined with boards, boxes, and barrels on either side. A rat was tipped out of a box, and Snapper had to catch it. He flung himself forward, and landed on top of it. There was a squeal, and he stood up with the rat in his hands. There were shouts of, "One, two, three, snap!" and Snapper bit its tail off.

Then a great burly man called Jasper stood on a tub, and another rat was brought. He took it out of the box and dropped it down the front of his trousers, which were tied at the ankles. Everyone gasped or screeched as the rat jumped around, making bulges, and the man made looks of agony and grasped at his backside. He finished by untying the cords and letting the rat run off into the yelling, scattering crowd.

I was separated from Dan and the girls. It was good to be alone, in the midst of this crowd. Some of the soldiers were mixing in, enjoying themselves. I was thinking of that other settlement, where once Two Songs pressed my face to her breast and I felt the thud, thud, thud, of her heart. I wondered now if we should have stayed, faced out those who wanted to drive her away, until she could have lived happily in the Eldo house for as long as she liked.

While I was thinking this way, with all the noise and movement going on around, I noticed three strange figures I had caught sight of earlier. Now, they were sitting under a tree, well down the left side of the street, beyond the other people, three women in black gowns, with black hoods that hid their faces. They sat with heads lowered, as if talking quietly or praying. I thought they might be nuns, come off the boat with the passengers who were now up the street enjoying themselves.

Then I noticed someone else. He was nearer, on the right-hand side of the street. He had his back to me. He had come out of a building and was crossing a gap to the next place down. He moved quickly, his left leg jerking out a bit to the side. My heart thumped and raced. It was Hurley. I glanced around to see that no soldier was looking, and went forward. But as I moved, Hurley's hoppity-hop had brought him to a door in the side of the house. He opened it, with a quick glance back, and went in.

ALICE TELLS . . .

★
★ ★

Chapter 31

BLACK CLOAKS

Dan excused himself from us because Lieutenant Malone wanted to talk with him. As we turned away, I noticed Cappy standing at the side door of a house. He knocked and waited. I wondered why he was there. He knocked again. After waiting a moment, he stood back into the road and looked up at the window. There must have been somebody up there, because a curtain moved. Then Cappy knocked again, and just after that the door opened. He gave a quick look around, as if he didn't want to be seen, and went in.

He hadn't noticed us, because of the people around. Two Songs was as puzzled as I was. Dan and Lieutenant Malone had moved off, so we went down the street and looked at the house. It was not a trim place. The boards were painted black, but the paint was dull, near gray. The curtains were drab and sun-faded to no color you could call a color at all. There were shutters, but some had slats out or were standing neither properly open nor closed. Mama would have said it was a house for Cronk's Ferry to be ashamed of.

There was no sign of Cappy, so after a minute or two we turned away. There were three nuns sitting under a tree a bit further down on the other side of the street. They looked kind of miserable, with their heads bowed, like in praying. There didn't seem much sense in needing to be praying in the midst of all the jollity, even if some of the fun wasn't all that special, like some idiot-looking boy biting off a rat's tail, or a great man risking his thingummy being bit by a rat jumping around in his trousers.

Two Songs looked even more puzzled than I was, but I didn't know how to explain about nuns or praying, so I linked arms with her and we went up to find Dan again.

The big man was up on his tub, with another rat making him hop. Dan was watching. We went up behind him. I said it was disgusting, but I was laughing with everyone else. Dan said it was disgusting but fun. I asked wasn't he scared. He said, "I hain't got a rat down my trousers."

A bit later, when Dan had to go about some duty, Two Songs said we should go to look for Cappy. We stood by the side door, not quite sure about knocking. Then we went out the front again and looked up at the windows. I thought someone moved behind a curtain.

Two Songs said she thought she saw Cappy. I said we should go back to the door and knock. Just then, there really was a movement behind the curtains. I saw Hurley. He shouted something, and struggled to open the window. It was the kind that slides up, and he couldn't budge it. He shouted and pointed, then Cappy was shouting too.

At that moment, I saw a movement at a ground-floor window, and a reflection of the three nuns. They had moved up the street and were now behind us.

They were not nuns, not women. They were three tall Indians, and one was tremendously tall. He was throwing off the black robe, which I could now see was really a cloak, running toward us, his face streaked with colored patterns. The window shot up. Hurley and Cappy were shouting that it was Long Shadow. I had never actually seen him before, but his picture was in my mind from what Two Songs and Cappy had said about him.

Two Songs was screaming, but the sound was cut short by the cloak thrown over her head. Muffled cries came from inside. The man had his hand and the black folds over her mouth. He lifted her in one movement and flung her over his shoulder, running. I saw no more than that because a cloak came over my own head. I screamed, but my scream was trapped in a mass of coarse cloth, and my feet were dragging on the ground as one of the Indians tried to rush me away. I tried to kick, but then I felt myself being flung upward and falling over his shoulder. His arm clamped around behind my legs, and my head was downward at his back. All breath was knocked out of me by the thump of his shoulder as he ran, and I could only moan.

The third man must have brought forward their horses. With the cloak still keeping me in darkness, I was flung across the front of a saddle. The horse began to move. I was pulled across the man's thighs as he put it into a canter.

Chapter 32

HATRED

It seemed like for an hour the Indians cantered their horses, only slowing to a walk a couple of times. As soon as we were moving, the man had to take his hand from my mouth. I tried to yell, but the only sound that would come was a long whimper, then another and another. The only way any sound would come was by fitting in with the horse's movement, and I could hear Two Songs making cries that were much the same. The only comfort in all that time was in knowing I was not alone in what was happening to me but that Two Songs was alongside. I soon began to realize that our cries were a way of telling each other that we knew we were not alone.

Long Shadow and his friends seemed greatly amused. My man suddenly gave his horse a slap, which made the animal jerk into a faster pace. Then he whacked me. My scream so surprised me, after a long time of whimpering, that I made another. The Indian laughed, and shouted something back to the others. They jabbered something to him and caught up as he let his horse slow. Long Shadow whacked Two Songs. She started a scream, but was able to stop it. I didn't know whether she was just refusing to scream for him or was trying to show me it was better not to give them the amusement they wanted. I told myself I would not scream again. I wasn't sure I could keep to that.

The darkness inside the cloak was complete except for a tiny gap where it was hanging down. I could see the grass speeding by, the outside edge of a hoof coming and going. When I screamed, my elbow jerked sideways against the man's haunches, and I felt the handle of the long knife at his side. As the horse pounded on, knocking my breath out with the thumping of my ribs, I grasped a fold of cloak in each hand. In my desperation, I thought that it would be possible to move my right hand inside that loose cloth and grasp the knife handle. Just at the right moment, I could slide the blade upward, then thrust it down with all my might into his thigh, or even plunge it sideways into his belly.

It was only a desperate fancy. I knew I was too scared to do more than whimper. I thought of my sister Henny whimpering outside the kitchen door when Mama had slapped her, and I knew I was a whimpering child. For a while I wanted to be that. I wanted to be home and whimpering with my little sister. I didn't want to be growing up, laid across a crazy Indian's thighs, with the pummel of his saddle hurting me, and my head hanging down sickeningly, and his reins-hand resting on me, maybe ready to whack again for his sport that I knew I could never really stop. But I could pretend I didn't know that. I could pretend the great knife could be in my hands. I could pretend the thrust into his thigh, the blood rushing up into my clothes, his scream, his fall sideways, the hoof cracking his skull, my struggle to throw off the cloak and pull my head up to the horse's neck, my hand finding the reins, my eyes open to the sky, looking around for Two Songs.

But it was only pretend. I knew the best thing was to stay safe, do whatever these crazy men ordered, try to keep them from hurting us, let them amuse themselves rather than become angry. Cappy and Hurley had seen what happened. By now the soldiers would be following us. They would keep their distance, wait their chance to take Long Shadow by surprise. But I wondered if anyone could ever take Long Shadow by surprise.

When we slowed from the canter, I could hear Two Songs talking to Long Shadow. He answered her roughly. He whacked her, and she checked her cry. He laughed.

She called out to me that he had allowed her to sit up, but that she still had the cloak over her head. Long Shadow said something to my man.

The man laughed, pulled my head up, then took me by the waist, lifted me like I was no weight at all, and sat me in front of him.

Just before we cantered again, the Indians talked, then my cloak was thrown off. The light was the brightest I had ever seen. The man's hands were huge, and he had no decency at all in handling me. I hated him for that. But I was out of the darkness. I could look sideways in the dazzle and see Two Songs having her cover pulled off too. Long Shadow had no decency either. But that seemed a small thing compared with what he might do to us, and with what he had done to Burkhart.

"Are you okay, Alice?"

I said yes. I asked if she was. She said yes. Long Shadow seemed annoyed that she was speaking English. He growled something to her and dug his heels into the horse's sides.

We cantered on. Several times I tried to see if the soldiers were in sight. The distance was hazy, and our dust hung in the air. When the Indian realized why I was trying to look back, he jabbered something to me and laughed.

We had turned away from the river. The sun was in our eyes, but still quite high. We were going somewhat west. When we slowed again, we crossed a shallow stream. The men drank water, and brought us some. We cantered on, more slowly, and came to another stream or another part of the same one. We crossed that too, and cantered on.

With the sun in my eyes, and the heat of the man's body behind me, and his breath hot on my neck, and, maybe, from the shock of all that had happened, I felt myself near to falling asleep. I tried to make myself fully awake by pinching my legs, but they seemed kind of numb.

I said, "Stay awake," aloud to myself. "Stay awake." The Indian grunted.

"Stay awake," I said. I said it over and over. Then I thought my lips were not moving at all, and I wanted not to care, because I was so tired. I knew I must not lean forward, or I might fall, even though the man had a hand half across me. I must lean back. Back against him.

I was falling asleep, leaning back against this man I hated, and the horse was moving on, like forever.

Several times I came partly awake, from a jumble of dreams, and the horse was going on and on.

When I woke properly, there was the sunset ahead of us. The horse was standing still. The man was dismounted, reaching up to hold me from falling. I looked down at his face. He said something, and I knew he meant I should let him help me down. I wanted to cry out my hate of him, but I let myself be lifted. He carried me and set me down against a rock. Night was closing in. I saw Long Shadow and Two Songs. She was sitting against another rock. He was crouching to talk to her.

Then he stopped talking, and listened. The other Indians were standing rigid, looking out into the shadows. Long Shadow took an arrow from his quiver, fitted it to his bow. I looked where they were looking. I could see nothing but shapes of the landscape. Then the head of a deer was a dark shape against the sunset. Then the top of its back. About thirty yards away.

Long Shadow took aim. I hated him. I wanted to cry out to frighten the creature away, but was shivering with fear. The bowstring twanged.

The head of the deer reared against the light, turned, and was gone, with a fading sound of hooves. But Long Shadow ran forward. He came back with a limp fawn dragging at his side.

He came to Two Songs, swung the little creature and

dropped it at her feet. He spoke a few words to her, then took his knife from his belt and dropped it, blade downward, on the fawn. It stuck in its side. Two Songs stood, pulled the blade out. She looked at me, then slid the blade from the delicate little neck, right through the belly, to the hindquarters.

I hated her, hated her.

Chapter 33

DISOBEYING ORDERS

Lieutenant Malone said I must stay at Cronk's Ferry until the soldiers returned.

"But, sir—"

"No damned 'buts,' boy," he shouted. "You stay here." He looked at Saucepan. "You can help Mister Partington sell saucepans."

I stood with Saucepan and the Cronk's Ferry people to watch the soldiers go. Corporal Dan said the army hardly ever chased after Indians. They just followed steadily until the opportunity for attack came. It might take a while, but in the end the Indians would become careless, leave themselves off-guard.

"Then we must attack when Alice and Two Songs won't be put in danger," he said. "I sure love that lil' gal."

I wanted to say something like that, but I said nothing. I watched him brush a corner of an eye. He said the horse's swishing tail had caught him.

He ordered the men to mount, then mounted himself. Lieutenant Malone joined them, bringing Hurley.

They had put Hurley in a crumpled uniform that didn't fit. They gave him a horse that was too high for him to mount with his crippled leg.

Someone helped him up. Corporal Dan gave him a rifle. He looked kind of happy in spite of everything.

Someone in the crowd said he was a deserter. Someone else said he was wounded at Gettysburg. Saucepan said Hurley was being given a chance to redeem himself. Someone said Saucepan used a ten-dollar word. Saucepan said the idea was worth more. I didn't know what either of them meant, but I thought Alice and Two Songs would be safer where Hurley was, wherever it might be.

Just before they moved off, Hurley looked back for me. I went forward.

"Thanks, Cappy, fer lookin' out fer me. I'll never fergit." He grinned. "Alice'll be back, perculities an' all."

I wanted to say something to him, but I didn't know what it was, and then the chance was gone. The little column of blue moved at a trot into the blue distance. A light cloud of dust drifted across the plain. I went back to Saucepan. It amused me to think "perculities" was one word he would never know.

Saucepan put an arm across my shoulders. "I'm tired of selling saucepans for today. Shall we observe life for a spell?"

We walked among the people. The feeling of the crowd had changed. The big man had a rat down his trousers again, but few were watching. We went to the man left in charge of the army supplies, and he gave us coffee. He said something about what Indians did to white girls.

"Most of those stories have no basis in fact," Saucepan said.

"You mean they ain't true?" the soldier said.

"They ain't true. A morsel of truth, a meal of exaggeration."

We went back into the crowd. There, too, much conversation was about the danger to Alice. A woman was saying that she knew of a girl taken by Indians and never seen again for twenty years. When she was set free, she had forgotten her own language, and wanted only the life of a squaw.

We heard a man telling some ladies about the punishment of army deserters. Some were branded on a hip with a branding iron in the shape of a letter *D*. Some were lashed and had their heads shaved. Some were shot. The ladies were giving squeals and gasps, like little children excited by a story.

"Have you known many deserters?" Saucepan asked.

The man stared at him, silent. The ladies looked for an answer, then looked to Saucepan, expecting him to say something more.

"Neither have I," he said.

The ladies laughed. As we walked on, Saucepan put his arm across my shoulders again. "Am I reading your thoughts aright, Cappy?"

"I don't know."

"That you and Cronk's Ferry are ready to part company?"

I said yes. He said he wanted to take his saucepans elsewhere. "Somewhere in the direction the soldiers have gone."

"But Lieutenant Malone . . ."

"Are you in his army, Cappy?" He slapped my shoulder. "Well, neither am I."

Chapter 34

QUARREL BY A CAMPFIRE

I helped Two Songs gather wood for a fire. There was not much to be found, so we had to make do with dead roots of shrubs and a few chips of buffalo dung that seemed as old as the world. We didn't speak. The men seemed not to think we might run off into the dusk, and hardly bothered to watch. They watered the horses in the stream, stood as openly to pee as their horses did, then sat to smoke while Two Songs cooked strips of meat on hot stones. The food was beginning to smell good, and I was hungry in spite of seeing the little deer slit and skinned. When Two Songs needed to excuse herself, she was as unashamed as the men were, but I was sure I wasn't ready to squat under their eyes, so I walked off until I was well away. Two Songs said something, and they laughed. I guessed she was telling about shyness.

The sunset was almost complete, only a last spread of red-gold light picking out patches in the dark country. I was startled by a sound close by, a kind of moan. It came again, shorter and sharper. I looked around. It seemed to be from an animal that might be dying. Then I nearly died myself, from shock and shame.

A man was lying alongside a low rock. He was under a blanket, but one arm was raised, moving against the rock to make me see him. I pushed my dress down the fastest in all my life, stumbled away, and fell. The man called something and stood up. The light caught his bony face and long white hair. I was on my feet again. I looked at him and gave a cry of shock. In a moment, my Indian and Two Songs were with me, looking at the old man. He said something. They recognized him. They talked, then led him to the fire.

Long Shadow was not pleased, but said the old man could eat with us. One of the Indians fetched his few belongings from under the rock. He talked a lot, in his high, shaky voice. We enjoyed the meal. I thought of the doe out there in the darkness, sniffing for her fawn, getting the smell of our cooking and not knowing what it came from. But I ate hungrily, anyway.

Two Songs told me what was being said. I was no longer hating her. I knew she had to live according to the ways she had learned. And I was less frightened now.

Long Shadow was taking us to the tribe. The old man said we must change direction. The tribe was moving all the while. He was very old and sick. They had left him to die, in the Indian custom. It was his own request. He could not travel day after day. He had no family left. He was not a Sioux, he was an Arikara, taken in a raid when he was young, and made a slave. Two Songs remembered him from her childhood. He was old then.

He had been lying against the rock for a day. It had been long enough to make him change his mind about lying there to die. He was feeling better. He could die later.

The men were drinking whiskey from a bottle left with the old man. Long Shadow was getting wilder, trying to make the others laugh. He danced as they clapped. He leaped the fire, pretending he was about to sit on it as he went over. The old man was greatly amused. He said he could do that trick when he was young, but he could do it better. He could get nearer the flames.

Long Shadow told him he could get nearer the flames now. Two Songs stopped telling me what they were saying. She shouted something at Long Shadow. He pushed her aside, and took the old man up, and held him over the fire. The old man yelled and struggled. Long Shadow laughed and held him closer to the fire. The other two Indians shouted at Long Shadow. He threw the old man aside. The three argued, moving off a ways.

Long Shadow sprang onto a rock, then to a higher one, then another. He stood looking out across the country in the direction we had come from. I wondered if he was looking for the soldiers. The other men followed him. Suddenly there was the twang of a bowstring. The old man was kneeling with the bow in his hand. There was a cry from the rocks, and Long Shadow fell. The others jumped lower, into the darkness. Two Songs gripped my arm. The old man was jabbering. He dropped the bow.

The two Indians carried Long Shadow down to the fireside. The arrow had gone through his thigh. The point stuck out. He writhed in agony. The two rushed at the old man, kicked him a bit, then picked him up by his hands and feet, and carried him to the place where I had first seen him. For a while he called out, his cries joining in with Long Shadow's as the men tried to take out the arrow. They used their knives to cut off the head, and tried to pull it through from behind. Long Shadow gasped in agony, but the arrow would not move. Then they stripped off the feathers, and pulled forward. Long Shadow screamed, and after two more pulls and two more screams, the arrow was out.

But the blood would not stop. It poured down his leg and up his leg, as he lay there writhing. The Indians fetched cord from a saddlebag and tied it above and below the wound, but still the blood came.

Chapter 35

WAITING

Two Songs tended Long Shadow through the night. Whenever I woke, which was often, because of the cold, she was sitting there with his head in her lap. Sometimes she was talking softly to him, like singing quietly. Sometimes she was touching water to his brow.

The men had found more fuel from somewhere, and the fire was still alight. I moved closer for warmth. The Indians were there already. The one who had carried me moved aside to make a space. Once when I woke, he was touching my head gently. When he knew I was awake and had not pulled away, he ran my tresses through his hand. I was too tired to care. Yesterday I had hated him, but now I thought he would protect me from whatever harm was out there in the darkness.

The thought came to me that the soldiers might kill him. Yesterday I had imagined killing him myself. But now I wanted him to be safe, to be gone before the soldiers came, to slip away without notice, to go and live happily somewhere, away from Long Shadow.

Perhaps Long Shadow was going to die. Two Songs was singing to him. I thought she was singing, but her voice was so low, hardly words at all. Perhaps it was a poem. Her voice was so sweet and tender. I thought of her talking to me in the bedroom at home, from her mattress on the floor. I was at home in my dream, and I slept until the sky was turning light.

The soldiers did not come. The men took turns to look out from the highest rock. When I excused myself, the old man was stretched out behind his rock. The men had not bothered to give him his blanket. He made no sound or movement. I went closer, but not close enough to be sure he was dead. I thought he was. He looked dead.

He had been going to die soon, anyway, I thought.

I asked Two Songs if Long Shadow was going to die. She said yes.

He had been moved into the shade of a rock. She was standing with her back to him. He seemed to be sleeping. There was a trickle of blood from fireside to rock.

She said it was better for him to die than to be taken away by soldiers. She was near crying. She said Long Shadow was a crazy man. I told her I thought the old man was dead. She said he was a crazy man too.

She said my Indian would go before the soldiers came. She smiled. "He like marry you. He say marry you, take you to Sioux people. I tell him no, you don't want."

"No, I don't want."

She reached out and held a hank of my hair. "He not crazy."

The Indians were getting the horses ready to go. They came to see if Long Shadow could be taken with them. Two Songs said he could not go. They said it would be better to die with his own people than with the soldiers. They would wait for him to die. Two Songs said she would stay with him. They should hurry away.

We waited all the next day, and the soldiers did not come. Long Shadow died when we were not looking. He slipped out of his life so quietly, like the man who had passed Cappy in his soft moccasins on his way to kill Burkhart.

We dragged Long Shadow to the place where the old man was lying behind his rock.

There was nothing to eat but small roots. We clung together in the night. I thought about Buffalo Sky.

Chapter 36

RAIDING PARTY

We made good speed, but stopped every little while to rest the horses. Saucepan said he thought the girls would be safe. Long Shadow wanted Two Songs for his wife, so he would not harm her. Two Songs would never be a good wife if he allowed harm to come to Alice. The only danger was that Long Shadow might take the girls somewhere away from his tribe where we would never find them.

Saucepan showed me his new Springfield rifle. He said he felt safer in his little cart if he had his tall, steely friend hidden on the floorboards. I showed him my derringer. He said that with guns you had to start somewhere. He said he knew a lady in St. Louis who kept a derringer hidden in her petticoats.

He lay back in the grass and laughed. He was good to be with. He was a serious man, but fun kept breaking through. I thought that he was like Hurley, maybe because something had gone wrong in his life and he had to make the best he could of it. I thought that Two Songs and Alice would be safer because of him, just as they would because of Hurley. I caught his laugh and fell back in the grass. Bessie sometimes said that when somebody talked about you when you were not there, your ears would go red. I wondered if the lady in St. Louis had red ears.

"Don't ask me how I know, Cappy," he said, and laughed some more.

That night we slept in the cart. It was cold, and I didn't sleep well. Saucepan's horses kept stampeding nearby, then the stallion and pony became restless too. Whenever I turned, pots and pans tumbled. We moved on soon after dawn and ate biscuits as we rode.

At midafternoon, we saw a cloud of dust in the far distance ahead. Saucepan said it could be a largish party of riders, probably Indians. We sidetracked into a small gully for safety and waited under bushes. The party went by with a pounding of hooves not far from the top of the gully. Saucepan judged from the sound that there were easily twenty horses. He said he hoped the soldiers hadn't met them. They could be a raiding party.

"Too late now for what might have been between the white man and the red," he said. "Too much greed, too many lies. It can only end in tears and blood."

We rode on in silence for a long way. I wondered if he

was thinking something he didn't want to tell me. I kept thinking of old Ebenezer Riley. "When the Indians come in thousands, which they will one day, Buck won't have enough wood to go around."

In the late afternoon, we saw the soldiers in the distance. They seemed to have stopped for the night. Two fires were smoking.

"Remember, we're not in Malone's army," said Saucepan. "We please ourselves what we do and where we go. We're grateful for his advice, but we don't have to take it." He trundled on a bit. "But if he offers a nice hot meal, we accept gladly."

When we rode into the camp, Lieutenant Malone was not in sight to show his feelings. Corporal Dan said he was in the tent in the center of the group. He was not to be disturbed.

Hurley saw us, and came hop-hoppity, with a huge grin. I introduced him to Saucepan. He was kind of polite and not saying much. I guessed it was because he saw Saucepan was a gentleman. Saucepan asked whether they had met the band of Indians. Hurley said, "Yes, we met 'em." Corporal Dan said there had been a skirmish. Two soldiers had been wounded, which was why camp had been made early. They would move out at first light. Long Shadow and the girls could not be far ahead.

A soldier had shot a doe. She had come so close, so

inquisitively, as if wanting to be friendly. He had hesitated to shoot her, because it didn't seem right. She might have a fawn somewhere. But his friend had said, "Now, shoot now!" He had pulled the trigger and felt bad afterwards because they soon discovered the doe was tight with milk. The only good thing to say about it was that, by the time we had the smell of cooking in the evening air, everyone was hungry, even the man who had pulled the trigger.

Lieutenant Malone ate in his tent. When he came out, with a book in his hand, he looked at Saucepan and me for a moment, but said nothing about why we were there, only that it had been a long day for all of us.

"And I have no need of more saucepans, Mister Partington."

He told Corporal Dan to assemble the men.

"I want to read something to you," he began. "It is from my entry in the logbook for today."

He opened the book, looked at it for a moment, cleared his throat, and read.

"At three-thirty we engaged a party of about twenty-five Sioux in an area that gave little protection. There was no cause for action on either side, but the Sioux were disposed to create a nuisance. An exchange of fire took place, with my company driven to take the cover of rocks and fire randomly. In this manner, two Sioux were killed and several probably injured before the marauders turned and continued southward.

"During the action Private Hurley acquitted himself with conspicuous courage, quite unlike the character described to me. Twice, in the face of close fire, and in spite of his disability, he moved from his cover to bring to safety wounded comrades, Privates Cotton and Walter. In this, Private Hurley showed a disregard for his own safety, in the highest traditions of the service.

"Accordingly, I take responsibility for a decision to treat Private Hurley not as a prisoner but as a member of my company, until, with the grace of God, we are able to return to the settlement of Buffalo Sky, where he will be honorably discharged as befits his age and disability. I have seen no more worthy an action by a soldier for many a day."

The soldiers cheered Hurley. I thought he would be grinning his pleasure, but he hid his face and cried. After a while, everyone went quietly away.

I went and stood with him, but I couldn't think what words were good enough to say.

Chapter 37

GONE

Two weeks later, I was riding with Alice the last mile to Buffalo Sky.

Two Songs, Saucepan, Hurley, and the soldiers were gone.

We had left Two Songs in the care of her chief. He said she could be the guest of his seven wives. I sat with Saucepan and Lieutenant Malone, smoking the chief's pipe with him. We were his honored guests. Saucepan told me afterward that the meal we had just been served was of the chief's favorite dog. He said that to give guests a meal of a greatly loved dog was the highest mark of respect.

Two Songs and Alice were in another tepee with the wives. Some were no older than Two Songs. When the chief passed us his whiskey, Lieutenant Malone told him I was too young. The chief laughed. He said something in his own tongue. Lieutenant Malone told me he had given me a Sioux name. It meant "Young Man Who Has Much to Learn."

The chief said he guessed Young Man Who Has Much to Learn would like to say a long goodbye to Two Songs. I had taken a little of the whiskey. It was like fire in my throat. One of the wives took me to the other tepee and pushed me among the girls. I wished I had stayed with the men. The little squaws were excited, pretty, and full of questions I couldn't understand. Alice laughed with them at my embarrassment. Two Songs translated, but at some things she shook her head.

When it all quietened, she was standing there looking at me with a sad smile. It was nearly time for goodbye. When the time came, I remembered how, before she left the settlement, we had gone to the place where she sat on the stallion for Burkhart's drawing. She had put her arms around a tree to show her feelings. Now, I stood in front of her, and we put arms around each other, and all the squaws stopped chattering.

I was thinking of that every mile of the way home.

Saucepan had taken his horse and cart on the river steamer at Cronk's Ferry. He said he would try his luck downriver. He would come to Buffalo Sky in the spring.

A day's ride from the settlement, the soldiers had forded the creek to take a shorter route to their garrison.

•

The men made sport of Corporal Dan's long goodbye to Alice. The wounded men had been taken on the steamer from Cronk's Ferry.

Hurley crossed the creek with the other soldiers. Lieutenant Malone said his honorable discharge would be even more honorable if it came from the garrison colonel. Hurley said he would be home in his outhouse before the winter.

Two Songs had given Alice her pony. Sometimes we rode side by side. Sometimes Alice rode ahead. I tried to think of her as she might look in a drawing. Maybe I would try to make one soon.

We came around the last hill. Something was wrong. There was a smell on the air, the smell there had been for days after Burkhart's cabin burned down. We urged the horses on and soon we saw the settlement.

It was no longer the place we had always known. Half of its buildings were gone. The rest stood charred or were strange and out of place without their usual surroundings. The Eldo house was still there at the far corner.

Alice looked at me. She wanted to cry, but no crying would come. She made a little moan and kept making it all the way along the street, past Dolly Emms's store, with its front broken open, past the broken-off gates of burned cabins, around the corner, and up the slope to her mother's house, and still no real crying could come.

I was glad she couldn't cry. I was afraid of trying to comfort her. Afraid because my own throat was near to letting out a wail of feeling I knew I must hold in check.

We went into the backyard. The kitchen door had been battered, the lock broken. A board had been nailed across to hold the door closed. It came away easily. The cupboard doors were open, shelves were bare. A slit sack of flour had spilled over the floor.

We ran through the house. There was nobody. Apart from the kitchen, everywhere was undisturbed. Burkhart's paintings were on the walls. There was even a sheet of music open on the piano.

Alice ran back to the kitchen and out to the outhouse door. I was close behind. There was a message written in pencil on the paint, small and neat, with lines drawn around it to make a page.

This seems to be the place for goodbye. We hope you find this. Indians came. Everywhere is burning. They came here last, then suddenly left. The cavalry came. Helping us to leave. Unsafe to stay. They will take us to settlements south. Come and find us. We shall wait for you. Come soon.

Your loving mama, Henny, & Bessie.

Then Alice cried. She leaned against the door, her face on her arm. I tried to comfort her, but she wanted to cry alone. I went in the house again. I wandered from room to room. I talked to Burkhart's pictures, like they were Burkhart himself. I said, "I took her back for you, I took her back to her people." His voice in the next room said, "Thank you, Cappy." I didn't believe it would be his voice, but I heard it again. I went in the room, and it came again from the next one, only a whisper. I knew I was hearing it only because I wanted it to be true. There are strange things. When I was with Two Songs in Burkhart's cabin after he died, I thought I saw him talking to the white horse up in the pasture. Bessie said we have to be able to believe things like that. It was true. We have to be able to believe things like that.

I flung open a guest room shutter and looked out across the place I had always loved. It was a place become strange, a place without people.

I wondered if they had all been able to get away, or if some had died in burning cabins or by arrows and bullets. Mama's note had forgotten to say.

My heart thumped. Over by the road we had come along, a bit to the far side of Dolly's store, someone moved. He crossed a space between shadows.

I waited for him to appear again. The place must be

Buck Riley's, but the house was gone. A building further back was the workshop, but the front was blackened. Then the figure crossed back. It was Ebenezer.

I bounded down to tell Alice. She had stopped crying, and was sitting by the outhouse wall, red eyed. She said she would come with me to see Ebenezer. Later we could light a fire in the stove and cook some vegetables from the yard. If we could eat tonight, we could start south in the morning.

She even smiled. "I let my tears come. Now they're gone, an' I know what we gotta do."

Ebenezer was sitting in the workshop, cutting up vegetables. He said, "Welcome home, Cappy . . . Miss Alice."

"Everyone else is gone, Mister Riley," I said.

"Gone."

"You ain't gone."

"No." He grunted, then grinned. "This is a stupid conversation, ain't it?"

"Stupid," I said. I felt my eyes filling up, felt ashamed.

Alice said, "It ain't a normal situation."

Ebenezer laughed. "Not quite."

"Why you ain't gone, Mister Riley?" Alice asked.

"My grave's here." He looked at me. His face was very old, but his blue eyes, and the lines around them, smiled. "I was the first come here. I'll be the last leavin' now. I gave it the name. Everywhere I looked, right up to the skyline, there was buffalo."

He said he had told Buck to leave. He had a life ahead of him. The Indian custom was for the old to ask to be left when they were too old to go on. It sounded cruel, but maybe it was sensible. He was trying it out.

He looked at Alice. "I guess you never heard of that, my sweet young one."

"No," said Alice. She glanced at me. Her eyes were bright with her secret. And she liked "my sweet young one."

Ebenezer lit his pipe and was thoughtful for a while. I told him how the Sioux chief had given me a name. But I thought he was not really listening.

"That little squaw of Burkhart. People didn't want her here. This wasn't the place for her. Now it ain't the place for them either." He was silent again, then went on. "And over the whole land the white man drove the red man off. Now, in this little place, the white man has learned what it's like to have to go."

I told him we were going south in the morning. He said, "Look out for Buck."

We told Ebenezer we would see him again. He said he had piles of vegetables for the winter, and his hens were laying as never before.

We went into Dolly's store and stood there. It was creepy. There was no food anywhere, no item that was ever for sale. Out back, the privy was still there. I remembered things I had thought about as I dug the latrine, like my mother "lost" on the prairie.

Going up the slope to the Eldo house, Alice put an arm around my waist.

"Ain't nobody can see," she said. Then, a few steps on, "You missin' Two Songs?"

I said, "Some."

"I'm missin' her," she said.